The Choice

To Alie
with all good wishes
Diana

The Choice

Diana Janney

Montano Books

London

First published in Great Britain in 2003 by
Montano Books
400/405 Kings Road,
London SW10 0BB

A CIP catalogue record for this book is available from the
British Library.

ISBN 0-9545827-0-5

Typeset in 11/16pt Goudy by
Kestrel Data, Exeter, Devon

Printed in Great Britain by
Biddles Limited, Guildford

To my mother, my late father, my husband
and all my other guardian angels
both in this world and the next

Part One

LILY

1

When I was a small child I had a friend whom no-one could see or hear but me. He was about my age when I first knew him – four or five – and he aged in parallel with me until he disappeared a few years later. I looked for him often after that, but alas, I thought, in vain.

He possessed the keenest, most intelligent eyes I have ever seen. If I saw them again, they would be how I would recognise him. He told me things, he taught me how to listen and when I was afraid or anxious, he gave me the confidence to proceed. He would emerge and disappear in the blink of an eye, and when he had gone, a white vapour would linger in the air where he had been like a cloud. Later, when I knew what it was to label concepts, I described him to myself as an angel.

He did not have a name, or, if he did, he never told me what it was and I, for my part, chose not to ask him. Names were not important to me then. What mattered was the sense, the essence, behind the reference, that part of a being which makes him or her a complete, unique individual, distinguishable from the rest of the world in the midst of a multitude of similarities.

That was how I knew him just as, presumably, that was how he knew me. I was not Lily Scott to him. Rather, I was a small slim child with a mass of straight blonde hair, an abundance of energy and enthusiasm, which could too easily be transformed into the opposite emotions of anger and despair. When that happened, he would usually be harsh with me. He did not shout, as I did. Instead he would stare hard into my wide-open eyes as if he were looking way beyond them to the inside of my head. At first, I would stare back defiantly, challenging him to a battle of wills, which it was beyond my capabilities to comprehend. Later, I grew to realise that this was a futile exercise, and a part of me gave in to him. Eventually I became appeased and mollified by the confrontations, which I recognised as his means of directing my spiritedness onto a different plane, more serene, more tranquil. It was not always the case that my anger or despair would disappear completely at these times, but they would take on an alternative perspective in my child's mind.

When I grew older, and adulthood began to wipe away a total recollection of my secret friend, I discovered other ways of experiencing similar perspectives. A great work of art – a Turner or a Matisse or a Rothko – would each in its own unique way heighten my sense of being, and awaken an appreciation of the spiritual side of existence, and in an instant the trivial aspects of life would be rendered insignificant. The voice of Pavarotti, the music of Chopin, or the words of Shakespeare were capable in their own ways of creating a similar response.

So they became my adult day angels – Turner, Matisse, Rothko, Pavarotti, Chopin, Shakespeare – or rather, not they, but the works of art which their names represented – their creations. In their works, I recognised as if in a living spark of genius, a fragment of what my young angel had left behind. Was that why he had come? Was his message complete? Had I heard all he had to say to me?

2

Where to begin? It would be easy to chart my life through all its varied stages, but would that really tell you who I am? I want you to know about me, to understand me, so that when you read of the choices I made it will be as if you yourself were making them.

Perhaps I should begin at the end, or what I believed to be the end. After all, that was really the beginning. Before then, nothing very remarkable had happened in my relatively short life. I can say that now because now I know what it is to experience a truly remarkable event.

Yes, there were times before it happened when I believed that there was something enchanted about my existence. Good fortune had blessed me with an easy life up to then, to such an extent that I did not understand what it was to struggle for anything I desired. And my security was not just financial, it was emotional too. I was loved and adored by my family as if the whole world depended upon my well-being. Perhaps their whole world did, I did not give it much thought. I assumed that everyone's life was the same. Sometimes it was as if I only had to wish for something to happen and before I knew it, it had become a reality. How foolish I was then. If only I had understood as I do now. If only I had not taken my good fortune so lightly. If only it had happened sooner.

I should have anticipated that my luck would run out one day. I thought it had when my father died. I was thirteen then. It had been my birthday the day before. My mother had organised a party for me. It was to be a surprise party, but I knew. I always knew. It was hard to keep secrets from me because I usually guessed what they were. The idea would just pop into my head unexpectedly, no matter how hard I tried to prevent it. Sometimes it would be in a dream – I would see my mother carefully wrapping a gold charm bracelet and placing it under a Christmas tree – and the secret would be over. On Christmas Day, I would try to look surprised when I opened my present, but she would know from my face that I had guessed again. It was as hard for me to hide my thoughts as it was for others to conceal theirs from me, only mine were written upon my face, whereas theirs were inscribed upon my mind's eye.

It was not until I was about nine or ten that I realised that this gift or knack of mine was a little out of the ordinary. It was my headmistress who had first inadvertently brought it to my attention.

"Lily Scott!" She had announced my name from the doorway of the classroom, which was filled with twenty-eight females of whom I was one. All eyes had turned from Miss Wellington to me as I jumped to my feet and hurriedly followed Miss Wellington along the corridor. Had I been a more confident child, no doubt I would have remained calmly in my chair at the sound of the booming voice, and boldly answered, "Yes?" to Miss Wellington's imposition. That would have been my mother's response when she was a child. She might even have ventured so far as to reply, "That's me!" As it was, my only concern was to remove myself from the room before any of the other girls spotted that my skin was reddening to the colour of a beetroot.

It was not that I lacked courage – I would not have hesitated to confront Miss Wellington, or anyone else, on an issue that mattered to me, if a confrontation had been required. But I knew my limitations (although I was secretly working on them every day) and one of them was that I was utterly self-conscious in a crowd. It is hard to imagine now, when I look back on the years that I have spent in my wig and gown, vociferating with all my worth in crowded court rooms up and down the country. Did I really manage to overcome my childhood weakness so easily, or did I become hostage to it instead?

At the time, I blamed my shyness on the fact that I was an only child, unused to conversing in large groups or fighting for attention amongst siblings who were ready to tease. I knew also that ridicule frightened me more than anything else in life, but death. Death as a concept, that is, rather than as a practicality. The physical aspects of dying did not frighten me at all.

Miss Wellington, or Boot as she was known to us, had pointed to a comfortable looking armchair in her study, to the side of her desk. I lowered myself gently without sinking back into it, and crossed my legs. They were unusually long legs for my age, and I felt particularly proud of them at that moment.

"Lily, I wanted to talk to you about your Form Prize."

I relaxed a little. From her expression, I had anticipated something hostile.

"Yes, Miss Wellington," I replied quietly and as politely as possible. "I am very pleased to be receiving it this year. And so is Ann Jones."

I did not redden this time. I was in my element: we were one to one.

"It was Ann Jones I wanted to talk to you about."

Then why hadn't old Boot summoned her out of Maths instead of me?

"You know that you are to be presented with your prizes – a book each – on Speech Day in two weeks' time, don't you?"

How could I fail to have known? I had been at the school for five years. It was the same routine every year. Did she think I was stupid?

"Yes, Miss," I smiled.

Miss Wellington got up from her side of the desk to come around to mine. I had never been this close to her before. She had more wrinkles than I had realised, and I was sure her hair was dyed.

"Lily, I wanted to have a little chat with you, just the two of us, about the books we have chosen for you and Ann."

I was not used to being spoken down to this way. At home, we were all equals.

"What about them?" I asked somewhat abruptly.

Miss Wellington manoeuvred her heavy body onto the edge of her desk so that her left leg swung to and fro while her right one stayed firmly fixed on the ground.

"I understand that you have been discussing the books you will be receiving with Ann."

Of course we had been talking about them. It was not every day you were awarded Form Prize. What did she think we would do?

"Yes, we have mentioned it." Did the Boot have nothing better to do with her time than this?

"And you informed Ann that she would be receiving a book on Wild Flowers, is that right?"

Did it really matter that I had guessed what book they had bought for Ann Jones?

"Yes, that's right. And I thought I would get a book on animals – probably dogs."

Miss Wellington stood up and returned to her side of the desk.

"Well, Lily!"

I was not sure whether it was a sigh or an exclamation.

"Would you like to tell me how you came upon this piece of information?"

"I guessed." How else did she think I would know? Did she imagine that I had broken into her study late at night and rummaged through her cupboards searching for clues, unable to bear the suspense for another two weeks?

"You guessed? You expect me to believe that you guessed the precise two books, out of all the countless possibilities, which you and Ann Jones are to be presented with?"

So it was a book on dogs!

"It's the truth, Miss Wellington."

Did she think I would lie? I never told lies. Lies made me feel uncomfortable, like looking at the sky through dirty windows.

"Lily!" She smiled. "I shan't be angry with you. I only need to know how you found out."

"It just came into my head one day. I didn't know for sure that I was right. I never do at the time. Not until later."

Miss Wellington stopped smiling and looked hard into my

eyes, as if she were looking for something she had missed, but knew she would not recognise even if she saw. I had never seen a look like that before, although I was to see it many times in the future. It told me something about myself which, until then, I had taken for granted: I possessed a unique gift, an insight which was sometimes beyond even my comprehension.

So, on the day of my thirteenth birthday it came as no surprise to me, when I arrived home at half past six, to find that our house was filled with schoolfriends clutching prettily wrapped presents for me. But there was something which even I had not anticipated – my father's absence. It was the first time in my life that he had not been at home on my birthday.

I did not need to scan the room full of familiar faces to know that he was not there; I sensed his absence, just as I could sense a pending thunderstorm from the drop in my body temperature. What I did not guess, however, was that he was about to die. In twenty-four hours' time, he would become a memory, which could never develop him further as an individual in my mind. Out of reach, out of touch, beyond communication, he would remain forever the sum of my experiences of him up to that day. If I were ever to hear anything new of him, which I had not heard during his lifetime, I would never be able to confirm or refute it as I would never be able to take the discovery to him for his response. He had become a finished book. I had reached the last page and all I could do was to take the book off its shelf from time to time and relive a part of it, recall a sentence, a thought which had once influenced me, when all its mysteries were still to be unwound.

I thought my luck had surely run out that day. Nothing could possibly be the same again. A birthday card arrived for me the

16

day after my birthday, the very day I heard the news in between my mother's gulps for breath. He had posted it in Moscow as soon as he had heard that his flight had been delayed. On the front, there was a picture of large, yellow sunflowers against a background of cornflowers. He knew that yellow and blue were my favourite colours. Inside, it read:

'Dear Lily,

So sorry I shan't be there for your birthday, but you know I shall be with you in spirit. Take good care of yourself and Mummy until I see you again as soon as I can.

Happy, happy Birthday.

Much love

Daddy xxxx'

I kept the card and used it as a bookmark. It went with me to Cambridge five years later and steadied me through three years of law books until I received my First. How proud he would have been of me – the only First awarded that year in my college. The card was frayed at the edges by then, and there was a teacup ring on the back of it. But it meant as much to me as when I had first taken it out of its bright yellow envelope, all shiny and new-smelling with a slight ink stain on the left hand side where he had closed it too quickly before the ink had had time to dry. The smudge was what made it part of him – he was always in a hurry. Even the stamp, stuck at an angle in the top right hand corner, reminded me of him. And the small, thin, spidery writing that sloped as it did to the right and went up at the end of each line was every bit as much a part of him as the photograph I kept by my bedside.

Yet, even then, my good fortune continued, albeit in a different form. My mother and I, God knows how, learnt to grow and develop the talents we had, until our lives had taken on new dimensions. Of course, we continued to mourn his absence, yearn for his presence, but his loss did not restrict our individual growth as I had feared at first that it might. In the midst of chaos, somehow order had prevailed.

I left Cambridge and turned my step happily and, I have to say, easily, to the Bar. There were many opportunities in 1993 for a Cambridge graduate with a First Class Law degree and two scholarships. I chose a set of chambers in the Middle Temple, where I had been called to the Bar, and a successful and lucrative career began. Perhaps the absence of struggle made it matter less to me than it should have done. Perhaps, that is, I continued to take my good fortune for granted. I did not give the question much thought at the time. I was too busy throwing myself wholeheartedly into what I believed to be a worthwhile career and, more importantly, one of which my father would have approved.

And then I met Harry. To describe Harry is almost like analysing a part of myself. I can barely recall life without him now, and yet, when it happened, that event which was to change my life forever, I seemed to accept his absence as part of a plan that I was not at liberty to comprehend – at least then. It is only in retrospect that I understand it, like stepping back and looking at a finished canvas covered with my brushstrokes, which I never really felt were within my control; I held the brushes, I mixed the oils, sometimes I even wiped out my work and began again, but I never quite knew why, what was wrong with it, why it had to be changed, why it was so much improved the second time around.

He was a lawyer too. We met when his firm of solicitors, in

which he was a junior partner, instructed me in a case. It was a negligence case and I was acting for the claimant. He told me later that I was the most formidable barrister that he had ever heard. I did not know then that he had heard very few, but that would not have bothered me. What was important was that I had impressed him with who I was and for some reason I wanted him to understand me completely.

Together we became even more formidable than apart. Perhaps it was our shared Celtic background pulsing through our young veins – I liked to think so at the time – our dual image was important to me then, I was so young, we both were. Shared goals mattered to us, especially in the face of our adversaries. No cause was too small for our common quest for justice. After all, that was what had drawn us to law in the first place. And if our beliefs were unpopular, as they often were, with those around us, we would not be deterred from finding an alternative route and continuing the battle.

It has to be said that on several occasions the battles were between ourselves. We had our own personal principles to fight for, and neither of us was easily swayed. Then the objections would become less reasonable, the arguments less subtle, the voices raised, and instead of eloquently phrased sentences, clearly articulated swear words would be used. Of the two of us, Harry was the quieter, although his beliefs were often much harder to influence. What mattered to me was not what he said so much as why he said it. Was he expressing a view because he thought it would irritate me, was he appearing not to grasp a point because it did not suit his view, was he trying to persuade me that he agreed with me when truly he did not? These were the questions I needed answering.

Our months together turned into years and eventually we married. It was to be the beginning of a long and happy life together. We talked of how many years we were likely to have. We agreed that Harry would go first, which would be easier because he could not live without me. I never really believed that, and I do not think Harry did either. I could see him adapting to a life without me quite easily – playing his piano, reading his books, walking in the countryside content with his own company. In fact, it hurt me sometimes to think that I was quite so dispensable. I did not tell him though, I knew what he would say:

"Wee daftie! I would not want to live if you were not there. Don't you realise that by now?"

Once or twice, it even occurred to me to test him – let him think somehow that I was gone forever and see what effect my absence had on him. But the scheme would have taken too much calculation and deceit and as I possessed neither of those attributes I gave him the benefit of the doubt and accepted that I was a "Wee daftie". In any case, what if he did go first? Did I really know how I would react to that? Didn't I need people around me more than he did? Wasn't I more vulnerable to loneliness? Everyone who had been close to me was in agreement that I became unbearable when I had too much time on my hands to ponder and allow my mind to follow every thought to its ultimate potential conclusion: if I were alone in our apartment, Harry was never just late, he was always dead or, worse still, unfaithful. If I had a headache and there was no-one there to tell, by the time Harry came home it would certainly have developed into a brain tumour. Was that how my days of widowhood would be spent, bravely overcoming one disaster after another until my time for departure arrived, suddenly, tragically when I least expected it and had not had time to prepare?

I think it was Harry who came up with the ideal situation. What if we were both to die at the same time, suddenly, with no warning. That way neither of us would have to suffer the pain of the other's absence, or the anticipation of death. Eighty was agreed to be the ideal age (in fact eighty for Harry was eighty-two for me, but neither of us ever referred to this). We would have spent more than fifty years together, time enough to achieve most of our goals, if not change the world completely. Our family, of which there would be one child and two grand-children, would be old enough to accept the loss as something expected (although they could never have guessed that we would have misread a clear black run and skied over the edge of a cliff, after so many years of experience in St. Moritz).

My mother, who would have died some twenty years before us, would look on from her celestial heights to see me tumble down a mountainside, gaining speed at the point where my path was intercepted by a cluster of pine trees. Behind me, dear Harry would fall heavily, lurching from side to side, attempting to break his speed with the strength of his once muscular arms, wishing he were forty years younger and cursing himself for his inability to protect us both from the fate that awaited us.

When it came, death would not be an end but a reuniting with those we had lost during our long life together. We would be still for a while, gathering strength for the next stage of our journey, then suddenly, hand in hand we would find ourselves in Paradise, much as we had looked when we had first met, the subsequent years having been wiped from our appearance as if they had never been, and the associated pain and suffering which had left their marks on us both physically and mentally, erased like sandcastles at the end of the day. Tenderly my mother and father would lead us to our new home, a mansion set in a garden of brightly-coloured flowers, where the sun always shone and angels flocked to greet us with unique renditions of their music. Harps would be played in abundance, with violins especially for me, and trombones especially for Harry. There would be laughter and a lightness of spirit without interruption as, free from anxieties and frustrations, we absorbed ourselves in moment after moment for all eternity.

But that was our future. The present was harder to contemplate. It moved us from day to day without taking us anywhere in particular. Like those around us, we knew what we wanted to achieve but we seldom attained that for which we strove. Our ideals were just out of reach, almost attainable, elusive to the point of frustration. Our life together was almost perfect, not quite. Our careers were verging on successful but with scope for improvement. Our home was in some ways what we wanted, but just out of our favourite location. Our holidays, although frequent, could have been longer. Our friends could have been more loyal. Our colleagues could have been more truthful. Our days could have been longer, our nights sweeter, our ambitions firmer, our promises wiser, our objectives clearer, our love calmer. But that was the way we were – back then, before it happened, before the pattern of our existence altered beyond recognition and nothing was ever the same again.

3

The year was 2002. The month was October. Harry and I had decided to take a holiday in the mountains of Mallorca. We had never been to Mallorca before. We usually stayed in the South of France when we needed to get away from London for a while. Someone must have recommended the village to us but I cannot remember who it was. Perhaps we had read about the hotel in a magazine. All I know for certain is that we were excited at the prospect of a peaceful week in the mountains at the end of an extremely stressful few months.

There was nothing remarkable about our flight to Palma. We sat together by the left wing of our aircraft. I was by the window and Harry on my right. I seem to remember that the seat next to him was empty. Harry took my hand in his as we took off and I looked out of the window, caught up in the speed of the event. I remember running my finger over a small platinum cross which I always wore around my neck; it must have been an automatic gesture as I was not thinking any spiritual thoughts at the time. I would like to say that I was, but it would not be true, so I cannot. In fact, I was wondering whether I could prevent my ears from becoming muffled by the pressure if I sucked hard on a eucalyptus sweet which Harry had given me moments before.

Moments. What are they in the context of a lifetime? The time it takes to cross over from one state of existence to another perhaps? From fear to elation, from happiness to misery, from hope to despair?

My next memory is of flying just above the clouds. That was the part I always enjoyed most. Their shape and texture mesmerised me and in a strange sense I was comforted by their presence, as if they were large fluffy white duvets which would envelop me in their softness if we should happen to fall through the sky. They made it easy to imagine that we were climbing ever closer to another sphere, somewhere purer and truer than the one we were leaving behind. I was content to think that I would not be subjected to the pollution and overcrowding of London for a week.

"I didn't think we would get away with all our hand luggage this time!"

As he spoke, Harry nodded his head in the direction of the overhead compartment, which contained our two full travelling bags. He knew how much it worried me to wait for our cases to come round on the conveyor belt at the end of a flight, so he preferred to bear the burden of our 'hand luggage' whenever possible in order to remove my fears. I laughed and gave him an unexpected kiss on the cheek.

"What was that for?" he asked.

"Nothing in particular," I replied happily.

There must have been food served during the flight, but I cannot remember it. Perhaps I was already asleep by then. I always fell asleep on planes. Once, as a child, some twenty years earlier, I had travelled all the way to the Philippines with my parents on a sixteen hour flight and had slept through the entire journey. It was a fortunate habit, especially during turbulence.

Turbulence. Was there turbulence that day? It was the fifteenth of October and there was certainly heavy rain when we boarded the plane. There may even have been a thunder-storm – or perhaps that was the child behind me kicking the back of my chair.

I must have fallen into a deep sleep, as I had a dream. Strange that I should still remember the dream. I dreamt that our plane had landed and Harry and I were walking off before everyone else. The other passengers were sitting quite still in their seats apparently unaware that it was time to disembark. We walked down the steps and into the airport, delighted that the sun was shining so brightly and the sky was clear blue. There were two queues at passport control in the dream. We chose the one on the right as it was smaller. On the left, almost everyone was dressed in dark untidy clothes. There was an old man crying and holding out his hands towards another old man in front of him who seemed not to hear him. Two children in tattered jeans and trainers were fighting with each other, throwing hard punches and shouting abuse. A young woman of about my age wearing a short black dress and patent black stiletto heels stood with her hand on her hip looking towards our queue. When she saw Harry, she beckoned to him with a long red painted fingernail. I was irritated by the gesture and wondered how Harry would react. He appeared not to have noticed her. He was looking to the front of the queue where a man in a black suit was checking passports. Harry looked anxious. Perhaps he had noticed the woman with the red fingernails after all. She was still staring at Harry, she made no secret of it. Maybe I should go across to her queue and confront her? No. She would enjoy that, whatever I said to her. She would know she had succeeded in irritating me. I decided to stay where I was and wait. Just then, Harry turned abruptly to face me.

"Our luggage!" he exclaimed, nervous of my response. "We have left it on the plane!"

It was as if he had said that the world had come to an end. I ran back towards the plane, Harry following behind me, but the steps had been removed.

"It's your fault!" I shouted at Harry, partly because of the woman with the red fingernails. "You are supposed to look after us, Harry. I should be able to rely on you."

Tears were rolling down my cheeks when I woke to find we were still in the air. Harry placed a comforting arm around my shoulders.

"You were dreaming," he said. "What was it about?"

"I cannot remember," I replied, which was true then. It was not until later that the dream came back to me, as we were walking through passport control. There was a woman in a short black dress in front of us and two young boys fighting behind us.

"She pushed in front of us!" Harry protested as the woman in the short black dress turned around and smiled at him.

"It doesn't matter," I said to Harry and then, remembering the dream, I added, "Let her go. We are not ill-mannered like her."

There was so much noise inside the airport that I feared my eardrums would burst. I could see that Harry was speaking to me but I had no idea what he was saying. I shrugged and pointed towards two open glass doors in front of us. Once outside, the noise stopped immediately. It was a curious sensation, to be surrounded on all sides by high pitched voices and loud chatter one minute and then total silence and solitude the next. The closest that I had experienced to it was diving into the silent depths of a swimming pool which was bustling with noisy children on its surface. But this was different. There was no apparent reason for the sudden silence. All we had done was to take a step outside through open doors. The crowd was still there, I could see them when I turned to look back over my shoulder – young and old, travellers of every race and description, jostling with each other for space and air, anxious and tired, no doubt, at the end of long flights from heaven knows where.

It suddenly occurred to me that I may have gone deaf, so I turned abruptly to Harry and said:

"Can you hear anything?"

"Only you," he replied and I smiled, relieved to discover that I could still hear.

Just then, an old man approached us. He was dressed in off-white baggy trousers, sandals and an open-necked shirt. His skin was brown and weathered.

"Mr. and Mrs. MacAllister?" he asked us, but it was more a statement than a question.

We nodded and climbed into the back of a large black limousine.

"I didn't know that you had arranged for a car to pick us up," I whispered to Harry.

"Neither did I," Harry replied.

Strangely, in retrospect, we were not concerned by our unexpected driver. Perhaps we assumed that the hotel had arranged for him to meet us, or, more likely, we were oblivious at that time to everything but our surroundings and each other.

"Just smell those pine trees!" I exclaimed, closing my eyes to inhale their aroma more vividly.

"And look at the poppies, Lily. Have you ever seen such a vibrant red? I wish I could freeze this moment and bottle it forever!"

I had seldom seen Harry as enthusiastic about anything. It was as if we were both looking at the world for the first time, with a child's eyes but with an adult's appreciation of how easily it could all be otherwise. The higher we climbed into the mountains, the more transfixed we became. By the time we reached our destination we were sitting in silence, clasping hands as if we were in danger of falling from heaven.

"Paradise on earth!" I said, conscious that my body was free from tension for the first time in months. I felt at that moment ethereal, spaceless, as if I had been granted a glimpse of that other world known best to poets and theologians.

In another instant we were pulling up to the front of our hotel. It was a large sixteenth century manor house, built in traditional Mallorcan sandstone, which formed a perfect backdrop for the infusion of pinks and oranges and purples, which clung to its walls. In the distance, far below us, a calm sea reflected the deep blue of the sky, its surface absorbing playfully the sun's rays and lending its tranquillity to a passing sailing boat.

As the limousine disappeared back along the hotel's drive, a small black cat ran down the twisted trunk of an old olive tree and walked serenely across our path, disappearing under an archway in the hotel's walls which led to an inner courtyard.

"That's lucky, isn't it?" asked Harry, laughing at the naivety of his superstition.

"It must be," I replied, and we walked arm in arm in search of Reception.

Three smiling faces greeted us from behind a large oak refectory table, which stood in the corner of a white-washed entrance hall with an old ragstone floor. On the walls hung textured abstract oil paintings, which complemented the hotel's blend of new and old. Two panelled windows stretched from the heavily beamed ceiling to the floor, their original shutters pinned back by hooks to reveal the beauty of the pine-covered mountains that surrounded us, and the medieval village which nestled on a hillside in front of our hotel.

I wanted to speak, to share my thoughts with Harry, but words seemed superfluous at that moment, a hindrance to the experience of being. I knew that as soon as I began to speak, part of the magic would disappear and become distorted within the confines of my definitions.

We were shown to our room by a dark-haired young local boy who communicated to us – I forget how, whether in Spanish or in English – that we had been given a most beautiful room. He was not exaggerating. In the centre of the room, a large open topped four-poster bed with hand-carved barley twisted oak posts framed a large white king-sized bed. Beside the bed, two long French windows led onto an ornate iron balcony beyond which could be seen, through the leafy branches of an old cedar tree, the sea. Ahead of us, another set of shuttered windows opened onto the aspect of the village, perched above us. At once, the eye was drawn to the village's focal point – the church.

Harry joined me by the window and we surveyed in silence our surroundings as we sipped champagne from silver-based champagne flutes. Eventually he said:

"There is something familiar about the place. I feel as if I have been here before."

I knew what he meant. It was part of the thought I had had by the window in Reception a few minutes earlier.

"Not with me!" I teased him. "Let's go and explore."

"You should phone your mother first to tell her we have arrived safely."

I dialled what had been my home telephone number for the first twenty-eight years of my life until I had married Harry four years before. Harry knew that my mother worried about me, especially when I was on an aeroplane. It was understandable, since my father had been killed in a plane crash. My mother had never re-married. As far as I knew, she had never been close to considering it a possibility. She had realised when she married my father that there was a risk that he would be killed – she knew the dangers that his occupation entailed, although she had had no experience of the Security Services before she met him and she did not understand exactly what it was that he did when he was away from her. I believe that she did not want to know and he preferred not to tell her too much, for her own safety as much as for the security of the country.

The first time I pressed the numbers I was met with silence. I tried again. I thought I heard a ringing tone, but there was no reply. Harry suggested that I ask reception to put me through, which I did.

"Hello?" I was relieved to hear my mother's voice.

"Mummy, it's me!" I spoke loudly as I was afraid it may not be a clear line to England.

"Hello, is that you, Lily? Oh God, please let it be you!"

"Of course it's me Mummy! What on earth is the matter?"

"Hello? Lily? Lily?"

My mother's voice drifted away with my name. I was alarmed now. Something was wrong. I turned abruptly towards Harry.

"She can't hear me, Harry. Something has happened. I can tell by the tone of her voice. You try and get through to her."

Harry took the receiver from my hand. There was still some kind of connection.

"Mary, it's Harry! Can you hear me? Are you alright?"

"Is that you, Harry?"

"Yes, it's me," said Harry, winking reassuringly towards me, "I'll pass you over to Lily. She was worried about you."

"Hello? Harry? Tell me you're safe! Is there anyone there who can hear me?"

It was then that we realised that, although we could hear her, she was unable to hear either of us. What was more, she seemed to be unusually alarmed by the fact. Clearly there was a problem. Our tranquillity had been short lived after all.

"She must have been thinking about your father's crash and that made her worry about you. I am sure that is all it is. If she were in any kind of trouble, she would get a message to the hotel somehow. She is a strong, determined woman. You know that."

"You are probably right, but I think I shall go down to Reception just in case she has left a message."

I have no recollection of making my way back to Reception; my next memory is of two faces, where previously there had been three, gazing at me from behind the large oak reception table. I had paid little attention to the receptionists earlier – my excited enthusiasm at our surroundings had rendered them superfluous. I had barely even registered their sex. Now, however, I noticed every small detail about them, and not just because they might hold the key to a confirmation of my mother's well-being. There was something odd about them. How could I have missed it before? Perhaps they were not the same people? Yet there was something about them which struck a chord in my memory.

They did not look Spanish in any way. Unlike our driver, whose skin was weathered and sun-worn, these two looked as if their skin had never been exposed to daylight. It was not white and unhealthy, though. Rather, it glowed with a translucence reminiscent of the cherubs depicted in Italian Renaissance paintings. That they were young males was not obvious either, for there was a soft femininity about their rounded features and large brown eyes, which had initially convinced me that they were women. In fact, it was not until one of them spoke – I forget now which one of them it was – that I understood them to be men.

"We have no message for you, Mrs. MacAllister." He spoke in a deep voice which, although quiet in tone, permeated Reception. It was as if he had guessed the question that I was coming to ask. He continued:

"You will find it difficult to get through for a while, but keep trying."

The two of them then looked at each other without speaking as if I were no longer there. I was not going to be dismissed.

"Is there a problem with the connection to England?"

32

"It is not just to England. It is a universal problem. Try to be patient."

This time, it was the other one who spoke. I remember now. He had fairer hair than his colleague, which he pushed back behind his ears to prevent it from falling forward. I noticed that neither of them spoke English with the trace of an accent, yet the way in which they punctuated their sentences gave the impression that they were not speaking with their native tongue.

They were intelligent men – I could see that in their eyes. I would go so far as to say that they were wise beyond their years. It was an expression which many had used to describe me since childhood, so it was not one with which I was unfamiliar. How reliable it was as a conclusion, however, would remain uncertain for us all, I supposed, until the day of judgement, if there were such a thing. I had often asked myself on what empirical observation the description 'wise' was based, especially in my own case as I had seldom considered myself to be the epitome of wisdom. Certainly I was intelligent; I could not have been top of my year in Law at university had I not possessed a certain degree of intelligence, nor could I have won so many cases as a barrister had I not the ability to utilise the intelligence which God had bestowed on me.

God. Now there was a concept which caused me even more difficulties than wisdom. A Being who was omnipotent, omniscient and eternal – without beginning or end. Was that not what my mother had taught me, particularly in those formative teenage years after my father's death when we had talked night after night into the early hours about the possibility of an afterlife? I found the idea hard to accept back then, I still did. And yet it was undeniable that there was something appealing about it, something which rang true at certain moments of my existence. Now for instance, when I stood surrounded on all sides by the beauty and simplicity of nature in its purest form. How could I doubt now that all this was God-given?

"It is truly beautiful, isn't it?"

The other one spoke this time, the one who seemed to know what I was thinking almost before I did.

"Yes," I replied, casting a glance out of the window. When I looked back they were gone. I noticed a door behind where they had been, which I had not seen before. I supposed it was their office – I could hear them talking together in an accent which I could not identify. All that remained of them was the strong fragrant scent of their aftershave.

That was when it first happened. For just an instant I thought I saw the secret friend of my childhood, sitting on the corner of the reception desk and smiling up at me with those warm, intense eyes of his. And then he was gone.

Had I found him again? I wondered. Was it possible I could see him as an adult too?

4

Our room was empty when I returned to it. Harry must have gone to look for me. And yet, I had not passed him on the stairs, and he had not come to Reception, where he knew I was heading. Then where was he? It was not like him to go off exploring on his own. We did everything together, Harry and I. We always had, right from the start of our relationship. We had even tried working together, but that had not succeeded as Harry was not as natural an advocate as I was. He had not been suited to the Bar and had returned, reluctantly, to being a solicitor. We missed each other terribly during the day but took every opportunity to share a lunch or tea or a drink during our working hours. After we had married, it was the same. Whenever he could, Harry would arrange his day so that he could spend more time with me, and every evening we would be together. Some of our friends had criticised us initially for spending too much time in each other's company. But it worked for us and that was what mattered.

I locked our bedroom door behind me and went in search of him. I knew where he would head first – the swimming pool. But where was it? I found my way outside through a small door at the foot of our staircase so I did not need to go past Reception again. For some reason, I wanted to avoid the glare of those two receptionists for the time being, at least until I was with Harry.

A narrow path made up of jagged stones which fitted together like an intricate jigsaw puzzle, meandered through the uncultivated landscape on the south side of the hotel. I followed the route, which took me past several olive trees whose trunks seemed invariably to separate in the centre and then intertwine like old married couples in danger of falling over without each other's support. At their feet, grass which was surprisingly green, grew in clumps, ready to cushion the black juicy olives which would fall from the stooping branches.

Ahead of me a line of palm trees restricted my field of vision, so I decided to climb a curving set of steps leading to a higher level where I hoped I would be able to survey the kingdom which I seemed at that moment to inhabit alone. My plan was more successful than I had imagined. With each step my hopes ascended new heights. I stood for what seemed like hours, but in reality must have been nothing more than minutes, wondering at the spectacular views that stretched out all around me.

Forests of pine trees carpeted the giant brown mountains which enveloped me, interspersed here and there with beige sandstone buildings which blended into the background like chameleons. Towards the centre of the valley, the village nestled quietly in isolation much as it must have looked in medieval times when it was first created. The only sign of life was the smoke which wafted into the atmosphere through the occasional chimney, and a dog barking playfully somewhere.

At the uppermost point, the eye was caught by the village's masterpiece, its crowning glory – the church. Even from my distance, I could sense the density of the rugged building and feel the security which its walled graveyard offered to those at rest within it. It was no coincidence that villagers and sightseers would need to use all their strength to ascend the steep surrounding banks, through winding cobbled streets, before they could reach the divine heights of this majestic place of worship. Nor was it by chance that there was nowhere in the village to hide from its moral glare. And once it had been reached, each worshipper, breathless and exhausted, would no doubt find the descent much easier than the climb. Unless, of course, it was their destiny to remain there for all eternity.

My thoughts were interrupted by the sound of splashing water behind me. I turned around to face a turquoise swimming pool carved into the landscape as if it were a work of nature. In the centre of the water, Harry's head bobbed up and down as he swam towards me.

"I thought I would find you here," I laughed, relieved that I was no longer alone in Paradise.

"The water's beautifully warm. Are you coming in?"

I threw off the few clothes I was wearing and jumped into the pool beside Harry.

"I missed you," Harry said, sweeping me up into his arms and swirling me around the water in circles.

"Is there no-one else here?" I asked, conscious for the first time that we were both naked.

"I haven't seen a soul since we arrived, except those three at Reception. How did you get on with them, by the way? Any news of Mary?"

"There are only two of them now, and no!" I said abruptly.

"Forget about it for a while and we'll try to phone her this evening when the lines will probably be less busy."

Harry knew that the best way to prevent me from worrying was to distract me, so he spent the rest of the day doing just that. When we had finished swimming, we lay on blue and white loungers by the pool, our bodies absorbing the sun's rays until we were ready for the cool water once again. When we grew thirsty, a waiter arrived as if by magic, with glasses of ice-cold white wine. Before we had time to give him our room number he had gone.

"Surely the hotel cannot be empty at this time of year," I whispered to Harry as he arranged a parasol over our heads. "Perhaps the others have gone down to the sea. I expect they will be back for dinner this evening."

I remember little else of our first day until Harry and I were sitting in the restaurant that evening. We were the first to arrive, so we had a choice of tables. We chose to sit under an olive tree at the side of the terrace which looked down to the sea. To my left, a large candelabra, some four feet high, held a dozen dripping candles which had formed into an interesting wax sculpture through burning in the gentle breeze for so long. In the background, classical music played quietly – Chopin at first and then Rachmaninov, I think it was.

Gradually other diners arrived. We watched their expressions as they walked onto the terrace for the first time and looked seawards at the orange-red sunset and the church framed with spotlights in the distance. Some chose like us to sit outside, others preferred the seclusion of the dining hall, which was a large, grandly-converted olive press.

We made a handsome couple, Harry and I. Harry had decided to wear black tie that evening. With his hair gelled harshly back from his face and his dark brown eyes he could have come from Italian descent instead of the Scottish borders. I had chosen a long silk lilac evening dress, which was cut off the right shoulder.

"You look like a goddess," said Harry. "Truly angelic. I always said you were an angel sent to save me. Tonight you look like one."

My hair seemed blonder than usual that evening – probably the result of a day's sunshine – and my skin had already begun to bronze. I was aware of the eyes of other diners upon us all evening. There were those who looked admiringly at us as a couple, and there were others who observed us with a look of resentment. It was not a new phenomenon, but one that was somehow accentuated that evening. It was as if every guest who walked onto the terrace where we were, fell immediately into one or the other category. Harry was not as aware of it as I was, and he tried to divert my attention from glaring eyes.

"This lobster is superb!" he said. "How is your foie gras?"

"Probably the best I have ever tasted," I replied, savouring my last piece on a corner of my brioche.

"Excuse me!"

We looked up to find an elderly gentleman at our table, leaning on a silver-topped walking stick. Like Harry, he was dressed in black tie, and although he must have been in his eighties, it was evident that he had once been a handsome man. Even now, he could be described as distinguished, and he had in his presence a bearing of style and gentility.

"I just had to tell you both how much pleasure it has given me watching you this evening. It is not often one sees a couple as handsome and obviously in love as you two. It has lifted my spirits enormously."

"Thank you," we replied in unison, but he did not wait for a response. He had turned away and was heading slowly out of the restaurant. All that remained of him was a tall, stooped silhouette and a shock of thick, white hair.

We walked through the gardens after dinner. It was dark now and we only had the moonlight to guide us. When we reached the front of the hotel, we paused by a large oak tree and danced. There was no music to be heard any more, so we hummed our favourite songs and swirled around and around and around. All I could see of Harry was his outline. A light breeze lifted my hair and blew back my dress. It was my favourite dress, I decided that there and then. Harry swung me under his arm and I pirouetted away from him for a second or two. Then I lost him. He must have been hiding behind a tree. It was not difficult to lose himself in the midnight darkness.

"Harry, don't be silly," I cried, a little alarmed. "Where are you?"

There was not a sound to be heard but my heartbeat.

"Harry, that's enough! I'm going without you!" I walked hurriedly in the direction which I believed led to the front door of the hotel. The moon had disappeared now and there were no lights from the hotel windows.

I was about to call out to Harry again when I heard the voice. It was nothing more than a whisper at first, almost indistinguishable from the noise of the wind brushing through the trees.

"Harry, is that you?" I asked, but I knew instinctively that it was not.

"Who's there?" I added nervously into the darkness.

"Do not be afraid," came the response. "I am here to help you."

"Who are you?"

"You will find that out later. Now I want you to do something for me."

In normal circumstances, I would have been terrified, but the voice was somehow calming and peaceful and I replied, "What do you want me to do?"

"I want you to make a choice."

"A choice between what?"

My last question was a mere thought which I had not verbalised when the voice answered:

"You will see. Come. I want to show you something."

Strangely, I did not hesitate to do as the voice asked and, even though I could not see him, or say from which direction he beckoned, I knew instinctively which way to go. Picking up the hem and train of my dress, I turned to my right and walked in the direction I believed led to the village.

In retrospect, I wonder at my daring or stupidity. Perhaps my desire to hold on to a belief in my childhood angel had been reawakened earlier that day in Reception. Perhaps it had never left me. Whatever the reason, I found myself groping through the darkness of a Mallorcan evening accompanied only by the calming sound of a deep voice and forgetful of my husband who must surely have been searching for me.

5

It was a sudden rise in temperature which first alerted me to danger. Either my body was responding to the adrenalin which had been pumping through it for the last few minutes or there had been a change in atmosphere. I grew so hot that I was afraid that I would faint. I felt an urge to turn around or call out for Harry again, but something compelled me not to.

"Where are we going?" I enquired nervously after some time had elapsed. I was met with silence. Eventually, the heat became unbearable and I fell to my knees. To my surprise, the ground was cold and damp. I raised my hand to my forehead to wipe away the perspiration, but there was none. Was I dreaming? I asked myself.

"No. This is not a dream, Lily," the voice replied.

He knows my name! I thought. Even my young angel had not known my name.

"I know everything there is to know about you," he went on. "You were born in Bamburgh, Northumberland in 1970, the only child of Mary and David Scott. You were a happy child, with many friends. You were extremely fortunate then. It was not until years later that you realised just how fortunate you had been. Your parents and grandparents adored you, and you loved them too."

He spoke the last sentence as if he were smiling contentedly.

"You have a great capacity for love. That is what draws people to you. You never understood that, did you Lily?"

"I thought that everyone was loved by their families the way I was. It was easy to love them in return."

Suddenly tears were cascading down my cheeks, the awareness of which made me cry all the more, and before long I was sobbing uncontrollably. I could see them all, as clearly as if they were right there in front of me, my father, grandma, grandpa, my great-aunt Hannah and Granny Scott. All of them gone several years before, leaving my mother and me as the only surviving members of our family, until I met Harry. One by one, they entered my mind's eye like actors on a cinema screen. For some reason, I pictured them younger than when I had last seen them alive, especially my father. His hair looked darker than I had ever seen it, without a trace of grey. He seemed broader than I remembered too. He was dressed casually in beige cords and a navy blazer. I had forgotten how handsome he had been. What struck me most about them was how joyful they all seemed to be, totally unaware of my presence, but absorbed in each other's company. It was as if Grandpa had said something amusing, and the others were laughing about it. Strange that I should picture them in this way.

"You took them for granted, didn't you? You still do, those who are left, that is."

I thought of my mother, sitting at home by the telephone, worrying about my safety, and Harry pacing up and down the hotel's terrace in search of me. Was it somehow my fault? I wondered.

"How well you did at school and university! You exceeded

even my expectations! It was your determination which impressed me. Do you remember when you first learned to play chess?"

"Of course I do. My father taught me how to play. I was four or five. We loved to play chess together. We would play for hours sometimes."

"You never gave up a game. It was not over until you were checkmated. As long as you had a piece left, there was still a chance of stalemate!"

My tears were replaced by laughter. It was a curious sensation, this mixture of emotions within such a short space of time.

"I like to see you laugh. You should have laughed more. You worried too much, you know. And most of the time, it was unnecessary. What a waste of life, don't you think?"

I did not answer, so he continued:

"I could never quite understand you. You are a complex soul. Paradoxical, I would say. You spent years worrying that this or that would happen – one of your parents would die, or you would be ill. You must have thought you had every illness under the sun at one time or another. And yet, whenever a tragedy or crisis actually occurred, you dealt with it admirably, without hesitation. The anticipation gave you more problems than the actualities, wouldn't you say, Lily?"

"You seem to know so much about me, you tell me!" I snapped at him.

"That is something else I like about you – your spiritedness! Fearless when angry, that is how I have often described you."

"Described me to whom?"

"You will see in good time."

"I would like to go back now. Would you please show me the way? My husband will be looking for me."

"Ah yes! Harry MacAllister. Your husband of four years. Born in Scotland in 1972. Two sisters he seldom sees and an elderly mother who does not understand him at all. Mary knows him better than his mother does. But then, Mary has a greater capacity for understanding."

"Will you help me get through to her?"

"You can speak to her soon."

"I just want to let her know that I am safe."

"Are you safe, Lily?"

I hesitated. It was a question I had been asking myself for some time now.

"Not yet," I answered finally, although I was not quite sure what I meant.

"Good!" He seemed happy with my reply. "Now it is time."

6

I used to believe that my young angel would protect me from harm. If ever I needed him, I thought, he would make himself visible and reappear in an instant, like Superman. Somehow he would know when danger was approaching, either because he had never really left me or because he possessed an innate ability to sense my fears. I had heard of twins like that who experienced each other's mental states even when they were spatially far apart. That was how I liked to think of us, as metaphysical twins bound together by an unspoken belief in each other.

But I was wrong in my belief. It was my first real tragedy which showed me my mistake. Suki, our dear, sweet Pekingese dog who had been a companion to me every day of my life, died suddenly at the age of twelve. She was two years older than me and I was young enough to believe that she would live forever. It had not occurred to me that she could die so young when I had my whole life in front of me.

It shook me at first when I realised that I was as vulnerable as the rest of the world and I looked in vain for my young friend. Had he not heard my plea? Was he with someone more needy of him than me? Had I displeased him in some way?

Whatever his reason, he had let me down and I resolved

never to look for him again. If he chose to seek me out one day, then no doubt he would know where to find me. The time had come for me to dispense with childhood flights of fancy and become an adult.

For a while after that, I laughed less, I worried more and I trusted no-one. It was easier than I had anticipated becoming an adult. But how much less enjoyable!

The magic had gone from my world; Suki was no longer there to lift my spirits with her enthusiasm for life and her games and her mischief, and my little angel had vanished like a dream. Sometimes I imagined the two of them existing together on another plane different from mine, unburdened by spatial or temporal constraints but free to materialise or dematerialise whenever they chose, kept alive only by their will to love. Both of them shared a capacity to love; that was what I remembered most about them. Whenever I was unhappy, Suki would come to my side and lick away the tears from my face until she saw me smile again. It was not that she was a particularly affectionate dog by nature. In fact, on the whole she disliked displays of affection – cuddles and pats were out of the question most of the time. Yet somehow she knew when she was needed, and she never once let me down.

Not like you, my young angel. But I cannot deny that you were capable of a strength of love and concern the like of which I did not experience once you had disappeared. Certainly I was cherished by my family even if, as the voice pointed out, I was guilty of taking their love for granted sometimes. But your affection was different. You owed me no duty. I was a stranger to you. I gave you nothing in return.

And now, years later, it has happened again. The magic has

returned. I sensed that it was on its way the moment we landed in Mallorca. I think Harry felt it too.

"Would you like to know his name?"

The voice was low now, almost a whisper.

"Whose name?" I enquired, half guessing the response.

"The name of your angel," he replied.

I shrugged into the darkness but he knew that the answer mattered nonetheless.

"His name is Michael."

"How do you know that?"

"Because I have seen him, too."

It did not strike me as strange that I was talking into the air about an angel who had last visited me as a child some twenty years earlier. In all the years that had passed since then, I had never breathed a word of our friendship to a living soul, not even to Harry. How could I explain him when I barely understood him myself? Besides, was he not a part of my childhood, a growing up experience that had helped to mould me into the adult I had become? What more was there to say about him – about Michael – than that?

Michael. The name seemed too ordinary for one as unique as he. I had hoped for a more unusual name, one that I would find difficult to pronounce at first.

"I would have preferred it if you had not told me!" I announced somewhat arrogantly. "Now he is limited in my imagination to ... to ...."

I hesitated, uncertain of my thought.

"To Michael?"

"Precisely!"

The voice was laughing at me. I felt foolish, a child again. I had to do something which would conjure up an essence of unpredictability which I sensed was lacking on my part. I refused to be a pawn in a game against a player whose pieces I could not see. In a gesture of flamboyance that was out of keeping with my personality, I kicked off my shoes and removed the heavy folds of lilac silk which formed the train of my evening gown, so that I was left standing in a flimsy short dress with an uneven hem. I felt unhindered, released from the material constraints which suddenly I realised had been restricting my movements.

"You have all the answers, what do you want from me?"

I stepped out of the circle of lilac silk like a lion freed from its cage by its keeper, but confused as to whether or not it would have preferred to have stayed where it had been after all.

"You need me, Lily, and I need you."

It was as if I were speaking to Michael again, but an older, wiser Michael. Had he grown up too? I wondered.

"Follow me for just a little longer and then you can go back. There is something you have to see first."

I walked on. It was growing lighter now. I looked back to see how far I was from the hotel, but it was nowhere in sight. I must have wandered further than I had realised. Surprisingly, I did not recognise my surroundings at all; where I thought I would find the village there was nothing but a steep mountain. It was darker than those I had seen earlier from the hotel and there were no trees growing on its surface. Instead of the ground being soft and clay-like, it looked as if it were made up of volcanic rock which had fallen away in craters here and there. It was unlike anything I had seen on the island. There was no prospect of vegetation or natural growth of any kind here. As I approached it, I feared that the earth would begin to crumble around me and swallow me up. I dared not speak any more in case the sound of my voice disturbed its status quo. Instead, I placed one bare foot cautiously in front of another like a tightrope walker. The ground became colder and colder. A fine layer of black powder covered my toes.

Inside my head, I cried out in pain, but outwardly I remained silent. He could not have imagined, the voice, how much torment I suffered in those first dark moments, the confusion which carried me first one way then the other. Several times I fell to my knees and scrambled in the black dusty surface on all fours like a newly born animal, fighting for some form of dignity against the odds.

Grasping at sharply pointed edges of rock I would draw myself up with the strength of my muscular frame and then down I would go again, crushing my kneecaps against the sooty ground. Sometimes I would feel the surface give way beneath my weight – that would frighten me most – and I would let out a small gasp. Did he hear me? Was he watching still from his hiding place? Was he laughing silently at my inadequacy?

I would give up. It was no good trying to go on further. If I lay on the rocky ground and slept, then someone would find me here eventually. Harry would come looking for me. Probably he had already set out with those two men from Reception – or was it three? They would have a knowledge of the area. They would lead Harry safely to me before long. Why had I listened to the voice? Why had no-one warned me? Why had my instincts not warned myself of the danger? Wasn't that Michael's role? I had given up relying on him a long time ago. Hadn't I?

I lay down on my back perfectly still, facing skywards, my hands by my sides on the rough ground. But there was a softness to the touch of my left hand that I had not expected to find. And instead of a coolness, I sensed warmth, a bodily, living warmth, like blood flowing uninterrupted through vital organs, coursing through veins, throbbing with intention.

I looked down to where my left hand was resting. I felt it move, but it did not move itself. There was something beneath it. I looked again. It was as if the ground were swaying from side to side in semi-circular movements. Left to right, right to left. Taking my hand with it. Although warm, the surface had a dryness about it which reminded me of the skin of our driver who had taken us to the hotel. There were pores, I was sure, large open pores whose oils had been sucked dry by years of heat and dust. I sat up abruptly and removed my hand from the moving earth. That was when I saw it clearly for the first time. The snake. It was a thick snake, about the width of my knee. How long it was I could not say for it camouflaged itself so well into the rough, black texture of the rocks. Its home, I supposed. But there was no mistaking what it was, and now that I had understood its presence I became aware of a gentle hissing sound emanating from its acid-white mouth. I pulled my legs and arms in to the wall of my stomach and buried my head in their vortex like a human cannonball. Then I let myself roll down the slope of the cliff, grazing myself cruelly on its rugged horns, which tore at my flesh and ripped at the remains of my lilac silk dress.

It did not take long to reach a resting point. The crevice was just about large enough to house me in my foetal position. I freed my arms and peered cautiously out from my hiding place. The snake had not followed me. I was safe for the time being.

My nerve endings released a surge of energy and relief into my feet which made them feel as if they were being tickled. I shook them hard, but I had been mistaken. My brain had misread the sensation, or at least its cause. My feet were not revelling in their escape, they were held captive by an army of snakes, all smaller than the first, their leader, no doubt, but of the same lethal concoction. The ground around me was alive with their wriggling bodies, clambering over each other, and me. There was nowhere for me to cling on to without taking hold of one of them too.

What should I do? Ask the voice to help me? Was that what he wanted? He said he had something to show me. Was it this?

"I have done as you asked. I have followed you here. Now will you help me back......... Please?"

There was no arrogance in my voice this time, only fear and humility. But it was not feigned in order to please him, to persuade him to help me. It was how I felt. Lonely, small and afraid, so very afraid.

I listened hard for his voice, but all I could hear was the hissing and subtle movement.

"Are you still there?" I pleaded. Silence again.

Then there was somebody coming towards me up the hill. All I could see from the outline was that it was a man. I tensed the muscles around my eyes to see more clearly. It was a young man, about my age, maybe a little younger. He seemed to have no difficulty mastering the rocky incline, but headed towards me as if he were walking barefoot along a sandy beach.

I forgot the snakes all around me, and the pain and the grazes and my fear. It was his eyes that I recognised, such intense eyes.

7

Whatever I had forgotten of him during the course of the previous twenty years came back to me in an instant. His wavy blonde hair, his pale blue eyes, his perfect skin, the way he lowered his chin and raised his gaze whenever he spoke to me. Of course, I had seen him as a child before, through my own child's eyes, and now he was an adult, like me. Strange that I had imagined him remaining the same, throughout eternity, a child with the mind of a sage, a cherub without wings.

Was he capable of taking on that child's form again whenever he appeared to other children? And when he helped the elderly, did his Adonis frame shrink and stoop with age, until he rose again on Phoenix' wing?

By the time he had reached me, the lower half of my body was submerged in a black sea of serpents, which rendered it immobile. It took all my strength to raise an arm to attract his attention. The gesture was unnecessary, Michael was already beside me.

As he fell to his knees, the sky blazed with a light so strong that I was forced to close my eyes. Then I heard lightning cut through the air like a whip. After that, there was a quiet calm which was broken by the sound of a voice I had not heard for many years:

"Look at me!"

I did not need to open my eyes to know that the snakes had gone. It was not just the absence of weight that told me, it was Michael's voice. I had forgotten how reassuring it was. I had forgotten how it would soothe me in the middle of the night, time after time, when I awoke from a childish nightmare, afraid to go back to sleep, and he would tell me that the shadows on my walls were not phantoms of the night, but fairies like Tinkerbell, sent to watch over me. He had taught me a prayer – how could I have forgotten our prayer:

"Help me sleep, Lord, help me dream
Of sunshine dancing on a stream
Of rainbows arched across the sky
And loving angels from on high."

"You remembered," he said.

"No. I forgot," I replied, "until you made me remember."

He seemed pleased with my response, happy to see me again. Or happy that I could see him again.

"How did you know I was here?" I asked.

We were walking down the hill together along a path I had not spotted before.

"He told me," was his only reply.

The voice. He must have meant the voice, but for some reason I said:

"Harry?"

"No, not Harry. Although he knows where you are."

It was not the answer I had expected to hear, and it shocked me for a moment.

"Has Harry spoken to you?"

It occurred to me that Harry must have been looking for me and ran into Michael on his way here.

"No."

He used to be more communicative than this.

"Then, does Harry know you too?"

I should have guessed that Harry and I would share the same angel, without even realising it.

"No, not yet. But a friend of mine has explained it to him."

"Explained what?"

"Why you are here."

I suddenly understood how the jury must feel at the beginning of a trial before the evidence is explained to them, and I wished I had been more understanding.

Presently we approached a lake, which was partially frozen where the sun had not yet melted the ice. It had grown warmer and warmer as we drew nearer to it and now I could feel the sun burning on the back of my head. All trace of the cold black rock had disappeared like a bad dream to be replaced by verdant meadows stretching as far as the eye could see. I was tempted to look back to verify that I had not been mistaken all along, but I feared Michael's reproach and refrained.

I had decided that it would be pointless to ask any more questions of Michael. I would wait for him to tell me what he chose in his own way and time. He had returned for a reason, that much I knew, and I was confident that it would not be long before I understood what it was.

The fact that it was light suggested it was morning, and yet the light had come so quickly, and the strength of the sun suggested early afternoon. I looked at my watch. Harry had given it to me as a Christmas present the year before. It was a beautiful delicate watch which had a black face with two diamonds, one where 12 and one where 6 should be. It was eleven thirty, exactly twenty-four hours since we had landed at Palma airport. How much had happened in those twenty-four hours! England seemed like a lifetime away at that moment.

"My mother!" I exclaimed suddenly. "I have to get through to her. She will be so worried about me. Won't you help me, Michael? Can't you tell her I'm safe?"

Michael stopped walking for the first time since we had set out down the hillside. We were standing by the side of the lake now. The ice had almost melted completely.

"Why don't you tell her yourself?" he asked, looking me firmly in the eyes as he used to.

"She is over there on the other side of the lake waiting for you."

I knew that Michael would not lie to me, yet I could not bring myself to believe what he was saying.

He was mistaken. Angels were not infallible, otherwise they would be Gods. And they were not. Half man and half God, they were somehow midway between immortal wisdom and mortal error, the product perhaps of an unhappy union between a divine being and an earthly individual, locked in an earthly world by the sins of the father whilst they strove to reclaim the status which their heavenly mother had denounced in order to be with her earthly soulmate.

I turned slowly around to face the lake with an air of contented cynicism. The ice had melted completely now. There was not even a sign of a recent thaw. My eyes, sensing move-ment, were drawn to the centre of the muddy-coloured water, where a white, regal-necked swan floated peacefully towards me, followed by an awkward eager line of her young.

I smiled. So Michael was speaking metaphorically! I should have guessed. I walked towards the water's edge and bent down to touch the water with the fingertips of my left hand. It felt warm and soothing. I longed to throw myself into it and feel the sun glistening on its surface, like the swan family. Could I? Would it be safe? Michael would know.

I looked over my shoulder to where he had been standing a moment before, but he had gone. I was not prepared for his departure so soon. After all, he had not yet revealed to me why he had returned. It was too soon for him to go.

I got to my feet and scanned the land all around the lake for a sign of him.

"Michael, where are you? Don't be silly! I know you are there somewhere!"

The words reminded me of those I had used to Harry by the front of the hotel the night before, the last time I had seen him and I continued:

"Harry – are you there?"

The silence was no surprise. I sat down on a bank of green grass tinged with blue, the scent of which overwhelmed my sense of smell so that for a moment all I could do was to inhale the heady aroma until my lungs were filled to bursting with the herbal essence. I closed my eyes and forgot about Michael and Harry and my mother. They would find me again eventually. In the meantime, why didn't I enjoy being me, Lily, on holiday on this beautiful island, away from the rest of the world? That was why we had come, wasn't it? To relax and escape from the pressures of everyday living in a city filled with pollution and overcrowding. What did it matter if I had wandered a little too far from the hotel? I was curious, was that so wrong? I had listened to that voice and lost my way. But I was safe now. That was all that mattered. Harry would understand. Besides, he could have helped me to avoid all this if he had only prevented me from going. But he had not. He had let me go. He only had himself to blame.

I was close to sleep, I could feel it stealing me away. I fought to hold on to the image of the lake before me, but it was slipping from my mind's eye. Now it was a bath in which I was being bathed by strangers. They did not attempt to speak to me and I for my part pretended not to see them. In an instant, the mountains around me had taken on the appearance of walls, and the sun had become a light bulb shining overhead. The strangers lifted me carefully out of the bath and placed me on a bed. It was a hard bed, covered in a white sheet.

When I tried to move my arms and legs and found that they were paralysed, I realised that I was dreaming. I had had this dream before. Sometimes it was accompanied by a sensation of falling from a great height. Usually, at the point when I realised that it was only a dream, I would wake up. But this time, curiously, I carried on dreaming. It was a strange sensation, to be caught in a dream, aware that I was living an unreality, but unable to restore my conscious brain to its natural state. I wanted to shout out, but I had no voice, I was barely able to breathe. Then there was someone at my bedside.

It was a familiar face this time. She was looking down at me as I lay motionless on the white bed. I could see that there were tears in her eyes. Her lips were moving as if she were speaking to me, urging me, but I could not hear her. She was holding my limp hand in hers, taking it to her mouth, kissing it while she stroked my hair with her free hand. It was my mother.

I awoke from my dream with a start and opened my eyes, but the sun shone so strongly that I was forced to close them again. I tried once more, squinting to avoid the glare. To my surprise, I found that I was in the shade this time. A shadow covered my whole body, although everywhere else was still in brightness. There were no trees around me – the area was quite devoid of anything that would cast a shadow. That made me curious. Was I still dreaming? Shielding my eyes with my right hand, and balancing my body in its cross-legged position with my left, I looked up. There was someone standing there, staring down at me, but who was it?

"Hello, Lily! I could not leave you here all alone. I had to come."

That was when I realised – Michael was infallible.

"Hello, Mummy," I said.

8

She had always thought of me as someone special, although she could not say exactly why. Her closest explanation was that there was something different about my thinking – not *what* I thought, but the *way* in which I thought it. Form rather than substance. Sometimes both. Others would think intriguing thoughts, I would create intriguing ways of thinking about them. That was what she enjoyed most about me. It took her closer to my father once he had gone, although I added something of my own stamp to his mind. Thank God. How predictable life would be otherwise.

She could seldom anticipate how I would respond to any given event – neither could I. Each new situation was precisely that, and I tried not to allow my mind to be restricted by past experiences. Of course, that was not to say that certain inductive leaps were not necessary sometimes, but on the whole, I preferred to think of those as premises rather than conclusions. That was what made me a good barrister – the flexibility of my thinking, my willingness to consider. She knew that, and I recognised it too. Although I had never dwelt on it until now.

Yet, when I saw her standing over me again, as if I were a child sitting helpless on the grass in front of her, it hit me as suddenly as a thunderbolt. In an instant I could understand what it was she had spent her life thinking of me, fearing for me, hoping of me, and I was overcome with emotion – happy and sad. I could see how I had let her down, raised her spirits, helped her, hindered her, underestimated her, overestimated her, taught her and learnt from her. And I knew that she understood it too – now, suddenly. She understood that it would not be important to me that she explained her presence there in terms of how she had come to be there, her journey to me, her anxieties on the way, whom she had met, what they had told her, what she had feared. All of those things mattered to her, not to me. What I wanted to know was *why* she was there, the all-important why – known better to man than any other species in existence. I needed an explanation, and my mother appreciated what it was that had to be explained.

"When I first heard that your father had died in a plane crash I did not believe it. They were mistaken. They did not know him as I did. He was a survivor. For weeks, even months, I waited for news of him. His body had not been identified, they could not be certain that there were no survivors. If he had died, I would have known. I would have sensed it somehow. We were so close, your father and I. He would have got a message to me, a sign, a glimpse of his new existence. He would not have just disappeared without a trace. But as time went on, I grew to accept that he had gone forever and that nothing I could think or do would bring him back in any form. He had gone com-pletely. There were to be no ghostly visitations in the night when I lay crying silently for his return, no sensations of his presence as we prayed in church, you and I, for his departed soul. He had vanished so completely and so suddenly that it was

62

as if his existence had been nothing more than a beautiful dream.

But then, I would look at you, Lily, our child, created through a bond that transcended the realm of the physical, mortal beings which we appeared to be. Then I would remember and rejoice in the existence we had shared together, we three. And I could bear his absence."

As my mother was speaking, I got to my feet and took her hands in mine. She did not respond to the gesture but continued to speak, almost as if I were not there.

"Whenever you told me that you were travelling on an aeroplane, I was filled with a terror so great that I could not sleep for days before you left, and when the time came for your take-off, I would pray to God incessantly for the duration of your flight. You never knew that, Lily, did you?"

She did not wait for a reply, but continued, looking straight ahead of her beyond me as she spoke:

"This time was no different from all the rest. At 10 a.m. I sat beside the portrait of your father in my bedroom and prayed. It was raining at the time you were due to take off. I had checked the weather forecast the night before. The rain was expected, it would not last long, the rest of the day was likely to be quite mild. I had hoped you would phone me from the airport before you boarded as you always had before. This time you didn't."

I remembered those moments before we had made our way to the departure lounge. Harry had carried our hand luggage, heavy as it was, I had told him not to use a trolley as that would have drawn attention to the weight of the bags and they might have been taken from us. We had stopped briefly at the chemist to buy some eucalyptus sweets to suck on the plane – Harry knew how much I worried about my ears on take-off since our previous trip when I had lost my hearing for twenty-four hours. I should have thought of my mother. We should have telephoned her before we left.

"When I did not hear from you, I telephoned the hotel. A receptionist told me you had not arrived."

She had over-reacted. It was understandable. I should have done more. How selfish I had become! She had come all this way to make sure I was safe, just because I had been too involved with my own thoughts to have time to consider hers.

"I tried to phone you, Mummy, but I could not get through. There was a problem with the hotel lines."

"I heard you – and Harry, but it was too late by then."

"Too late? For what?"

She looked at me for the first time since she had begun to speak. She was anxious now. I knew her well enough to realise that. She gripped my hands tightly, pulling them to her, and said:

"You were already here."

"Then why were you still worrying?"

She was silent as she contemplated what to say next. I wanted to reassure her but somehow I could not think of the right words. Eventually she went on:

"What time is it, Lily?"

I looked at my watch as I had done a little earlier that day. The two small diamonds, one at the top and one at the bottom, still shone at 12 and 6. The hands still pointed on the black face to 11.30. They had not moved at all.

"My watch must have broken. It has stopped at 11.30."

"The time you were due to land in Palma."

She looked afraid and relieved at the same time. It was a curious combination, one I had never seen in her before.

"Don't you know, Lily? Don't you understand?"

She was almost pleading with me now. I put my watch to my ear to listen for sound. I was panicking. I needed a distraction.

"I can't hear anything. It's dead," I murmured, avoiding my mother's gaze.

"No, Lily. You are."

9

There had been a thunderstorm shortly before we were due to land. Our plane had been hit, and exploded on impact with the runway. The news report had said there were no survivors.

She was alone when she heard the television news. She could not be certain then that it was our flight – there had been no mention of the flight number. There was an emergency number, which she rang, but the line was engaged. She picked up the receiver again, and dialled our hotel, but there was only silence at the other end. In despair she had called my name into the receiver, praying to God at the same time that it would be me. For a split second she even thought she heard my voice, then Harry's, but she must have been mistaken; her desire to hear us must have clouded her reason and she could not trust in her instinct at such a time. She tried the hotel again. A receptionist answered this time. Mr. and Mrs. MacAllister had not arrived at the hotel. Mary replaced the receiver and threw herself face down onto her bed.

She knew her limitations, she was a strong woman – she could almost hear Harry reassuring me of that. But the death of her only child would be too much for her to bear, the misery that it would invoke in her heart too great even for Mary Scott to rationalise and grow from. There had been events in her life which she had fought hard to overcome, injustices which she had struggled to comprehend, friends who had let her down, and sometimes she had questioned the reason to go on living. But, through it all, there had been me, there had been Lily.

I had given her a reason to continue. And even when I had disappointed her, her love for me and her desire to protect me from harm had kept her going. She had to be there for me just in case I needed her. And she was. It did not matter whether it was the middle of the night or she was sick in bed, if I had a problem, she would devote her entire energy to helping me resolve it.

But from the moment she had heard from the receptionist that we had not arrived at the hotel, she knew. There was no point in trying to convince herself, as she had when my father had died, that she was mistaken. I was her child, and every atom in her body told her that what she feared more than anything else in the world had become a reality.

Eventually she dragged her empty body downstairs and poured herself a double Scotch. She did not like Scotch. It was there for her guests. She poured herself another. It numbed her consciousness sufficiently for her to fall into a heavy sleep for a while. When she awoke, the pain hit her even harder than before. There was not a single person to whom she wanted to turn – the only people she wanted were dead.

She ran to the portrait of my father and gently traced the outline of his face with the fingers of her right hand, until his image was blurred by her tears. Then she fell to the ground and buried her sobs into the palms of her hands. Deep inside her chest she could hear her heart pounding blood furiously through her veins, the very blood which had gone into my creation. Was it possible for her somehow to transfer that energy which had once united us, into my crushed, lifeless body? Could her strength keep me going until I was found? If she concentrated hard enough, would my brain sense the urgency of her plea and be revitalised?

Every question she posed was met with a darkness inside her head that was cold and foreboding, like the constant, unbroken sound of a heart monitor when there is nothing more that anyone can do.

She wanted to die at that moment, she prayed aloud for it, but death did not come. It seemed ludicrous to think that there could ever have been a time when she feared death, such was her longing for it then.

She got to her feet again, so that she stood looking into my father's skilfully painted face.

"Help us, David! Please help us! Lily and me," she implored of the static image. But his silence was as deathly as my own.

The moment I grasped what had happened to me, I saw it all as clearly as if I had been there. No. More so. For, not only did I see my mother's state of anxiety, I felt it too, as if she were me. For the first time in my life – if I could still refer to my experiences as my life – I knew what it was to suffer another person's pain entirely, not from my perspective but from theirs. That was what made it so different from anything else I had known. It was as if I had a complete vision of every second that had led to that time in my mother's life, without being restricted by my own reactions. Was that what Michael was experiencing whenever he looked hard into my eyes?

"You should not have come here just for me," I said solemnly.

"Look again, Lily. It was not my decision. I wanted it to be, but the choice was not mine to make."

She drew me to her like I was a child again and kissed my forehead. She was relieved, I could see that. But why wasn't I? Did my number of years on Earth mean so much to me?

"There was so much more I wanted to do with my life. Thirty-two is too young to die! At least you were able to spend all those years with my father and have a child. Harry and I were not so fortunate. Our life together was just beginning. We had plans for our future. We had mistakes to rectify. We had potential to fulfil."

I looked down at my lilac dress and relived my last moments with Harry as we had danced together in the moonlight, so happy with each other. It had all seemed real at the time, like an idyllic holiday. But now it had turned into my worst nightmare. How could that be? Was it so easy for the future to destroy the past? Or were they one and the same now that we had moved onto this different plane?

"We have to find Harry!" I said, or thought, the two actions having become confused.

"You go alone, Lily. There is something else I need to do."

She smiled at me and I guessed what the something was – she would look for my father. I wondered whether I should stay with her, but she seemed not to want that, so I decided to set off alone. But in which direction?

It occurred to me for the first time that I was still assuming that my existence was governed by spatial and temporal constraints. But surely that could no longer be so? Hadn't I given up a life of hours and days and years? The ageing process was denied to me now. I would never look at myself in a mirror and see a time-worn face looking back at me, or wonder what my future had in store. There could be no future, just as there could be no distance through which to travel. For distance entailed space, finite space, with beginning and end, and I had passed through those barriers. I was a free spirit now. Wasn't I?

"No. Not yet, Lily."

I had not expected to hear the voice again. I assumed that his role was over. He had led me from paradise to hell and back again. I had made my choice at the moment when Michael had returned to me and the snakes had disappeared. That was what the voice had meant, wasn't it, when he had told me that he had something to show me? Hadn't he said then that the choice was mine?

"Yes, I did. You are right. You never forget words, do you, Lily? They are very important to you. They give you a sense of security. But do not confuse the meaning behind them."

"Then what choice were you referring to?" I asked.

"You are here for a purpose. There is someone here who needs your help."

"My help? How can I help anyone here?"

I was intrigued by the request, perhaps even flattered by it, but it seemed out of place. What could I do that Michael or one of his friends could not do a million times better?

"You can use your God-given talents, your brain, your intellect, your persuasion in argument and your capacity for looking into the hearts of others and seeing what even they do not always see about themselves."

"Who do you want me to help?"

"A young woman whom you will meet soon. I have told her all about you."

"What does she think I can do for her?"

"Nothing at all. She is convinced that no-one can help her."

"And you think she is wrong?"

"It is up to her, just as your decision is up to you."

I felt as if he were deliberately leaving it to me to draw out of him what he wanted me to do. Did he know already what my answer would be? Was it part of his plan to let me believe that I had a choice?

"What do you think I can do for her?"

"There are those who believe that she has committed a crime, a very severe crime. They think that she should be punished for it, the way that others have been punished by the wrong that she has done to them."

"And do you think that she should be punished?"

"I believe that she has been punished enough – by herself."

I was curious now. She sounded like the kind of defendant I had enjoyed representing at the Bar. A woman who may or may not be guilty of a crime of which others were keen to accuse her. And, even better, she had a conscience!

"Is there to be a trial?" I asked, as the pieces began to fall into place in my mind.

"Yes, there will be a trial, although it will not be the kind of trial that you are used to."

"And will you be the Judge?" I enquired hesitantly.

"No, Lily, you have misunderstood the purpose of the trial. I have judged her already – a long time ago. I shall not be the Judge this time. She will."

I was confused. It did not make sense. Was he playing games with me?

"You said you wanted me to help her, so I assumed she would be on trial."

"You are right in a sense. Her soul is on trial. She believes it is lost. I want you to represent her in a way which will persuade her, and others, that it is not."

His words were still unclear, although I was beginning to glimpse his meaning.

"How can she be the Judge and the Defendant at the same time? Won't that entail a conflict of interest?"

He paused, and I feared that I might have asked too much. Then the silence was broken with:

"You use your mind well, Lily. I admire the way you follow thoughts through in a logical manner. That is one of the reasons why I chose to entrust you with this task – if you are willing to accept it. The soul you will defend, if you so choose, is not as practised in rational, abstract thought as yours. She has an intellect – as you will soon discover for yourself – but her intellect is limited by being too closely harnessed to her own experiences and emotions. She needs to learn to stand back, and observe herself, her soul, from an objective viewpoint. It is her only hope for salvation. That is why I want her to be the Judge, so that she can listen to what you have to say about her soul, her actions on Earth, her responses to her situation, as if she were hearing about someone other than herself. That way, she can judge her soul more fairly. Will you do it, Lily? Will you represent her soul?"

I needed time to reflect, but time was not something I had any more. I sensed that he knew what my answer would be, not because it was predestined, but rather because I had already decided.

"Very well," I announced with a mixture of pride and excitement, "I shall do it! Who is she?"

"You will have heard of her. Everyone has heard of her. Her name is Eve."

10

I had never considered myself to be a particularly religious person. I had attended church regularly as a child, but later it had seemed unnecessary in order to be at one with God, assuming that there was such a Being, and I was not convinced of that anyway. In fact, my closest experience of a spiritual nature had been my friendship with my young angel. And he had let me down. Thereafter, I had limited my spiritual responses to by-products of my senses – works of art, pieces of music, literature, Nature in its purest form. If anything could have persuaded me of the existence of God, it was they.

That was not to say that I did not yearn for a proof upon which to rely in my logical mind. But there was never enough certainty for me. Eventually, I gave up the search and satisfied myself with what life as I knew and experienced it had to offer.

I had never read the Bible from beginning to end, only sections now and then. I could not even say how many books there were in the Old Testament. But I had heard of Eve. Adam and Eve. First man and first woman from whom we all descended, wasn't that what they said?

I racked my brains to remember anything I could about the woman whose spiritual salvation had been placed in my hands. It seemed strange to think that she knew more about me than I did about her. Eve, one of the most famous women of all time, had been told about me, Lily MacAllister, a nobody with quite a good brain, and a brief career as a junior barrister behind her, very much behind her now, with a loving husband and a devoted mother, and a capacity to, how had he put it, to look into the hearts of others. What could I possibly do to save Eve?

She had been created from Adam's rib. That was why she had been called 'woman', taken out of man. Alone they had lived in the Garden of Eden, husband and wife, blissfully happy in each other's company and unashamed of their nakedness. That was how God had created them, and that was how God liked them to be – pure, unselfconscious, loving and trusting of God their maker and of each other.

Many trees had been made by God to grow in the Garden of Eden, but there was only one tree from which Adam and Eve had been forbidden to eat. That was the tree of the knowledge of good and evil. If they ate from it, they would surely die, He had warned them.

Eve had been tempted by a scheming serpent to eat fruit from the forbidden tree, and Adam in turn had eaten the fruit too, which his wife had given him. From that moment, they had become conscious of their nakedness, which they had concealed with fig leaves.

It was their self-consciousness, which had made God aware that they had broken His command, and He had punished them and consequently all Mankind accordingly. Then He had driven Adam and Eve out of the Garden of Eden.

That was all I could recall of them. It did not strike me as a great deal upon which to build a case, either against Eve's soul or on its behalf. Clearly, I needed more information.

75

"Michael will introduce you to her." The voice interrupted my thoughts.

I was glad to see Michael again. His presence always made me feel safe. And I was sure that I could rely upon him to be honest with me.

"Michael, what is she like?" I hesitated to ask the question.

"She is a little like you; young, intelligent, insecure, curious."

He knew me so well. Did he know her just as well? I wondered.

"I expect you have met Adam, too?"

Somehow I could not imagine them being apart; a reference to one of them almost invariably included a reference to the other. That was probably how people thought of Harry and me, as inseparable. Yet, the one time when Adam should have been there with Eve, to protect her from evil, he was not. She had been on her own when the serpent had tricked her. Why, I wondered, had she wandered off alone at that very point? Or had the cunning creature been waiting for the right moment to challenge her beliefs for some time? I would have to find out.

"Adam was a very good friend of mine."

I had never seen Michael look so downcast. He looked as if the very essence of all his beliefs had suddenly been challenged and he did not know how to respond. I left a silence long enough for him to fill if he so chose, but he did not. Instead, he pointed to a shady area ahead of us, framed by drooping branches clad with heavy green foliage and brightly-coloured flowers – roses, irises, jasmine, all manner of sweetly scented shrubbery, which formed an interwoven arch through which a young woman could be seen, seated on a wooden garden bench, deeply absorbed in a book she was reading.

She must have heard us approaching, for she looked up abruptly and her book fell to the ground. In an instant, Michael was at her feet, kneeling to pick up the book and place it on the seat beside her. She smiled when she saw him. I recognised the smile. How well I understood it. It was born of relief and security in his presence. Then he did something I had never seen him do before; still in his kneeling position at her side, he lowered his head so low that his chin touched his chest and thus he remained, unmoving, for what seemed like a long time but may only have been a moment.

The woman, seemingly oblivious of my presence, gently placed a slender right hand on his left shoulder, as if she were bestowing a knighthood upon him. The action took me by surprise and I half wondered whether I should retreat and hide behind a tree out of their way. Yet had I not been brought here to this place whatever it was specifically to meet this woman? Had Michael forgotten that?

As if he had read my mind, he raised his head and got to his feet, turning around to face me as he did so.

"Lily, come and meet Eve!" he called out to me, almost in the tone of a command.

I stood still, uncertain what to do next. It seemed a long way to cross through the flower-clad archway, although I had already convinced myself that distance no longer existed by necessity in this other place.

"Lily. What a beautiful name! Like the flower." She spoke so quietly that I could barely hear her. But her intention was clear to see; she wanted to put me at ease.

Normally, when I met a new client, I was the one who put them at their ease. It had become something of a challenge to me over the years. I could understand why outsiders might be intimidated at first by the formality of the legal profession, with its procedures and rules and legalese. And a courtroom is an austere place, even to a trained lawyer. But somehow I managed to make my clients feel that they had someone to represent them who was on their side, who saw them as real people with feelings and fears rather than mere points of reference in a legal argument. But suddenly, I felt like the client. It was a new sensation.

I took a step forward. I could see the cover of the book she had been reading. It was Paradise Lost.

"Have you read it?" she asked. Wasn't I supposed to ask the questions?

"A long time ago," I replied, looking towards Michael for support.

"Did you enjoy it?" she continued.

I had not thought of the book since my school days when I had studied it for 'A' level English. Strange that it had not come into my mind before, when I had been trying to remember everything I had ever read about Adam and Eve. How could I have forgotten Milton's epic poem? It had moved me to tears at the time.

"Very much." The words seemed a lame response to the question, so I went on:

"Milton wrote it with such vision, as if he had been there with..." Dare I say it? "With you and Adam in the Garden of Eden." It sounded so personal. Was I intruding too soon? Was it my imagination or had she flinched when I mentioned Adam?

"He was too kind in his descriptions of me." Did she speak sincerely, or was she looking for compliments?

What had Milton said of her? I concentrated hard until the words started flowing back to me, like water in an opened dam that had been stagnant for too long:

'...her heavenly form
Angelic, but more soft and feminine,
Her graceful innocence, her every air
Of gesture or least action, overawed
His malice, and with rapine sweet bereaved
His fierceness of the fierce intent it brought.'

The poet was correct in his imaginings; there was a certain air of innocence about Eve. It was easy to believe that the serpent may have doubted his malicious intent for a moment when he met with her in the Garden. But she was not a fool; quite the opposite. In fact, she struck me on first impression as a woman who was keen to understand everything that was going on around her. Her dark eyes darted speedily from one observation to the next, taking in each minute detail upon which they fell.

But what struck me most about her was her hair. That was the only feature about which I had felt certain before we met – her hair would be long, very long. After all, she had lived a natural life in Paradise in every sense of the word, hadn't she? And every depiction of her I could recall portrayed her with hair long and thick enough to cover her nakedness. Yet the woman who sat before me had hair that was short and unkempt, and looked as if someone had taken a pair of scissors to it and hacked it off. She must have seen me observing it for she attempted to straighten the strands around her small face with her right hand as she said sorrowfully:

"I used to have beautiful long hair like yours." It was the second compliment she had paid me. I was surprised, especially as it came from a woman. I wondered whether to say something positive back to her, but I thought she would see that as patronising. So instead I did what I had always done in an awkward situation – I changed the subject.

"I'm afraid I know very little about you. I should know more. I'm sorry…" Why was I apologising? How was I to know I would be asked to help – how was it Milton had described her – 'much-humbled Eve'?

But I should have read more, learnt about God's first created woman. She was part of my ancestry, after all, we were all descended from her, if we were to believe what the Bible told us. And surely the fact that I was here at all lent credence to that theory! Not that I was entirely sure even now where I was. If this were Heaven, then why would I need to save Eve's soul – it would already have been saved, wouldn't it?

Michael read my thoughts once again and answered:

"Don't you know yet? You are in Purgatory, suspended between two states of existence. That is why you have not quite given up the temporal experience of existing as you are used to it. You will be here for a while before it is decided where you will go next." He looked from me to Eve then added: "And Eve, too."

Eve covered her ears as Michael finished speaking.

"I do not want to hear any more about decisions and your after-life! I have told you already, Michael, my mind is made up. It was made up long ago, only you will not believe me!"

Tears were rolling down her pale, fragile cheeks and disappearing into the corners of her open mouth. Without thinking,

I rushed to her side and threw my arms around her neck, drawing her to me as my mother had done with me many, many times.

"There is no need for you to be afraid any more, Eve. I am here to help you."

11

All the while, Michael stood over us, watching our every move. It was hard to believe that he was the same angel who had visited me as a child. Yet there was an aspect about his countenance which had not altered. His face bore a strength and dignity, which gave an impression of a warrior or leader of men. I could imagine him going into battle with a sword in his hand, driving back the enemy with the force of his presence.

"Michael is the greatest of all the angels," Eve said proudly when she saw me watching him. "He led all the others against the rebel angels. You must have read how he fought against the dragon?"

"I didn't realise; I thought he was just my secret childhood friend. I did not even know his name until I came here."

We spoke of him as if he were not there. His silence had created a barrier between us, which was welcomed by us all. It was time for Eve and me to do the communicating.

As if to emphasise the barrier which had emerged between Michael and us he moved a little away towards what looked like a willow tree in the background where he hung his head low like the floppy green branches which he caressed.

Whenever he wandered from my side, I felt myself start to panic in case he disappeared again. Sometimes I thought I saw the beginnings of a cloudy white vapour encircling him but when he remained constant, I realised that it was just my wild imaginings. Nevertheless, I continued to watch him intently, just in case.

"He comes and goes when he pleases. There is nothing you can do to prevent that."

Eve's voice interrupted my fears and brought me back to her. Perhaps it was the immediacy of my line of vision from Michael straight to Eve that first made me aware of the similarities in their appearance. It was not just the opaqueness of their skin and their rounded open faces. There was something more fundamental than that. The closest description I can offer is that they gave an impression of enquiry with every atom of their being, as if an electric current charged incessantly through them forming a circle of energy which made them alert to every sight, sound, smell, touch and motion which entered their field of experience. Looking at the two of them at that moment, Michael and Eve could have been angelic twins, born of a parentage into which I would not dare to pry. How different I must have appeared to them! A mere mortal who had somehow managed to transcend her own bounds of mortality without even realising it!

Why couldn't Harry have been here with me? He would have reminded me of how special I was too. Hadn't he always thought of me as his guardian angel? Sometimes I had even believed it to be true. In a way, I suppose I was. I had helped him through so many difficulties in his life, steering him onto a more spiritual way of existing than he had known before he had met me. Wasn't that what Michael had done for me too? What more was there to being an angel than that after all?

Encouraged by this thought I sat down next to Eve and took the book from her hand saying:

"What part are you reading?"

I grew confidence from the knowledge that I had chosen to sit with my back to Michael. Eve pointed to the lines she was reading:

> "Lament not, Eve, but patiently resign
> What justly thou hast lost, nor set thy heart,
> Thus overfond, on that which is not thine.
> Thy going is not lonely; with thee goes
> Thy husband; him to follow thou art bound;
> Where he abides, think there thy native soil."

I read the words quietly to myself before I spoke them aloud. I could sense Eve's eyes upon me as I uttered them. I wanted her to approve of my presentation of what was clearly important, vital to her. If I spoke with anything less than genuine expression, she would sense it immediately. It was not a difficult task; Milton's choice of words surpassed criticism. I read with clarity and I hope empathy.

Eve beamed at me as I handed the book back to her.

"You understand!" was all she said.

"The person addressing you in those lines was clearly very close to you. But I forget – who was it?"

Eve seemed uncertain how to respond to what I had thought to be a straightforward question. Before she had time to speak, someone else answered for her.

"It was I!" said a voice behind us. I turned around to face Michael.

12

I was disappointed when they both disappeared. There were so many questions I had wanted to ask them. Somehow I had not imagined Eve would come and go at will, if it were at will. But where had they gone? Where did Michael ever go? Instinctively I cried out to a voice which might not have been listening to me:

"What do you want of me now? I can't help her if she's not here, can I?"

There was no response. I tried again, louder this time:

"Who are you anyway? Why do I never get to see you? Are you God? Or do you want me to think you are? You could be the devil for all I know, teasing me and joking with my soul. Just like you did with poor Eve. How was she to know what you were up to with your craft and sophistry? She believed what you told her, was that such a crime? She did not think she was doing wrong. She was curious. Curious for knowledge. What was wrong with that?

And now you think you will fool me too, do you? That I will do what you want and believe it to be my own choice? Well, you have chosen the wrong woman this time, I know the difference between good and bad, I have experienced them both already. I am a woman of the twenty-first century, not a wet behind the ears child of nature. I have seen your type in the dock before. Bad through and through, always trying to make trouble, to pervert justice, to expose goodness and truth as a lie! I shan't let you do it this time, do you hear me? I shan't!"

I was trembling so fiercely that the ground seemed to shake beneath my feet. I got up from the bench where Eve and I had been sitting and ran towards the floral archway through which I had entered. Once on the other side, I realised that the ground was in fact trembling. More than that, it was breaking up. All around me, cracks were emerging which started like narrow slits but before long were wide enough for me to fall into. Suddenly it was dark again. There had been no warning. There was never a warning of anything here. Like disjointed dreams with no beginning or end, just a series of events and reactions, with the only binding force being me.

It seemed as if every time I found myself completely alone I was caught up in some kind of danger and my surroundings altered dramatically: a beautiful warm evening in an idyllic environment had changed into a chilling darkness on a threatening rock surface; a peaceful sweet smelling garden had been transformed into a sombre, earth-shattering place of desolation as suddenly as the disappearance of Eve and Michael. Had my peace of mind become contingent on the presence of others? Was it they who restored serenity to an otherwise perplexed mind? It was a possibility. After all, nothing was real any more, was it? I was a spirit now, not the physical object I had thought myself to be. I had given up that option on the aeroplane.

Then what was I seeing around me when I thought I saw a garden and a seat and a book and a rock and an hotel? And how was it that Eve and Michael and Harry had seemed like the finite beings I was used to seeing, with hair that I could touch and clothes that I could feel and bodies that I could embrace?

I could be certain of nothing any more other than that I, Lily MacAllister, was experiencing something. Everything else could be the creation of my imagination. But for so long as I believed myself to be experiencing something, I could be confident that I still existed in some form. As to the others, they may well be the by-products of an overactive mind, a memory of my past or a desire for a future. Somehow I had to find out.

As I had been thinking those thoughts, my surroundings had changed once again. All was calm now. The thunderstorm had subsided. Darkness had been replaced by sunshine and ahead of me an imposing sandstone building stood arched in a vibrant rainbow with colours that melted into each other like a Turner.

I walked towards what I had once believed to be the entrance of our hotel. The hallway was just as I had remembered, the same paintings on the walls, the same views from the long windows pinned open with their original shutters. There was even the same old oak reception table in the corner of the room. Only this time there were no smiling faces to greet me from behind it. This time the hallway was empty. This time I was alone.

If I were ever to see Harry again, then surely I would find him here, where I had left him.

Part Two

HARRY

13

I could not imagine life without Lily. She would never believe that, though. No matter how hard I tried to convince her, she could not understand just how important she was to me. That was one of the reasons I loved her so much. I had never met anyone as gifted as Lily, yet she was the only person not to realise it. She knew she was intelligent – she had certificates to prove that to herself – and she had eventually recognised that she had a unique knack of anticipating what was going to happen sometimes. That, too, was easy to prove to her. But she could not accept that she became utterly indispensable in the lives of those she chose to influence, or, if she ever did believe it for a fleeting moment, she never understood why. For my part, I was not eloquent enough to persuade her, and in that respect I fear I failed her.

If I had my life to live over again I would never fail Lily in anything. I would be the man she had always wanted me to be, I would never need a second chance. But then I am a mere mortal, not an angel such as she.

That was what I would call her, my guardian angel. That was how I thought of her always, even when she lost her temper with me in response to a perceived wrong or injustice on my part. Then the fiery side of Lily's nature would prevail, and she would take on the bearing of her Scottish ancestors, warriors renowned for their fearlessness and courage, crusaders for truth and justice, conquerors of wrongs. And I, who had never cared what criticisms others had levied at me, would listen to every word she had to say, for no-one had ever mattered to me as she did.

If the day had ever come when she had walked out on me, I doubt that I would have been able to carry on. My life would have been meaningless, I would have wanted to die. Not that I believed strongly in an after-life. But to picture myself carrying on the same life without her, playing my piano, going for walks, eating in our favourite restaurants, reading a book, listening to music, all of which I could picture myself doing without her just as I had done before we met, filled me with a realisation of how fine is the barrier between joy and despair, emptiness and fulfilment. I would happily have swapped fifty years of life without her for one day with her. Perhaps that would be what it would take to convince her. Perhaps that was why it had to happen.

I wanted so much to be perfect for her, but was I good enough for her? What did she really know about me, after all? I had told her nothing at first of the bad side of me, the lies I had told and the women I had let down. To Lily, truth telling was vital, a necessary ingredient of a happy relationship without which she would be unable to function. Nothing I had ever done wrong would be as bad to her as the sin of lying about it, I was convinced of that. But did I really know her well enough to be sure how she would react?

I swore to myself that I would never do her wrong. I owed it to her to give her the truth she needed, and if I lost her as a result, then I only had myself to blame.

I began by confessing to her everything I had ever done which I considered to be a wrong. Lily listened as I spewed out every seedy indiscretion, every illicit thought, every thoughtless transgression that I could recall and of which I was suddenly as ashamed as she. Why had they not concerned me before I met her? I asked myself often. How could I have sunk so low?

Her responses were seldom as I had anticipated. Sometimes, she would listen in silence, like a priest in a confessional, as I laid my soul at her feet for her to do with as she chose. Other times, she would cry deep, uncontrollable sobs like a wild animal.

But what influenced me most of all was her ability to make me think things out clearly for myself. It was as if she recognised instinctively that what mattered was that I should reach my own moral conclusions rather than that I should be given them by her. Of course I knew that in many ways she was a better person than me, and her very presence in my life influenced me accordingly, but at the same time, I grew not just by her example but by my own self-discovery which she guided very often with questions which she left me to answer.

Lily. My guardian angel. My salvation. Could it be possible that she was sent to me in order that I might be saved? God knows what would have happened to me if she had not entered my life. I was heading downhill rapidly then, both spiritually and physically, I see that now. How many more bloody fools are there like me in this world, blindly heading towards disaster without anyone around them bothering to point them in another direction? I was the lucky one and I did not take my good fortune for granted.

That was an area in which I could truly say that I was a better person than Lily. She was one of the most fortunate people I had ever met, yet she acted as if her good fortune were to be expected. Her mother, for example. Mary loved her daughter with an unselfishness I have never known, before or since. There was nothing she would not have done for Lily's well-being. It mattered far, far more to her than her own happiness, which very often she sacrificed for that end. The depth of Mary's affection for Lily was obvious to anyone who knew them. Anyone, that is, except Lily, who would constantly doubt her mother's motives and test her level of loyalty to the extreme. Yet, even when Mary passed every trial that was put in her direction, Lily could only respond as if it were her right to expect it.

She was like a child, sometimes, an adolescent child, yet at other times she was the wisest person I have ever known. "But how many have you known, Harry?" would be Lily's response.

The truth was that I had known very few people in my life before Lily. I had grown up in a small, close-knit society on the Scottish borders where every villager knew every other, not only by reference, but through a detailed awareness of the minutiae of each other's lives. Not that there was anything particularly interesting about anyone else, but whatever there was to say was exaggerated by audible whispers, deep intakes of breath and high-pitched intonations.

Naturally the word 'wee' was used frequently: "Have you heard about wee Angus Barnes?" "Do you know the rumour about wee Maggie Baites? What a silly wee lassie!" It was a useful wee word whenever the speaker wished to cushion the defamatory blow just enough to be coaxed into continuing, without gaining a reputation as a trouble-making gossip, which, of course, they were.

My mother and my sisters were no exceptions. I was brought up with stories of how the scandalous new minister had chastised members of his congregation whom he had caught gambling or drinking, how his modern young wife had been seen wearing a wee mini-skirt more than three inches above the knee, which was entirely inappropriate for a wee woman of twenty-six with a wee bairn and married to the minister, how it had been said, confidentially, that Mrs McFee had cheated at the W.I. quiz night. All of which was said by way of announcement culminating in a sharp, abrupt nodding of the head, just once, and a tightening of the lower lip which, in my mother's case, caused her chin to double in size as it sank down towards her heavily protruding chest.

As for my sisters, the intonation was the same, but their statements were punctuated by loud tutting sounds combined with a raising of the eyebrows heavenwards, as if in search of spontaneous divine chastisement to be imparted on the poor wee souls whose lives were more blasphemous than their own. After all, there were not many of their contemporaries who looked after their mothers the way they did, who gave up social lives in order to be available whenever they were needed, and how important it made them feel to be needed when the rest of the world chose to pass them by.

Even their own brother had chosen not to spend time with them, the fact of which gave them a great deal to bemoan with our mother. I had deserted them in favour of England, I had given myself airs and graces, I had been influenced by more worldly contemporaries.

Introducing them to Lily was like casting Grace Kelly in an episode of Emmerdale. They did not know whether to applaud my success or commiserate my future which, surely, would come to a sad end. You could see she was a flighty young thing, too much passion, not enough moderation. In no time I would be back in Scotland, broken hearted and forlorn, to be greeted by my mother and sisters with open arms, like the prodigal son.

Happily for me, their hopes were in vain. My visits to Scotland became less and less frequent which, in a way, I think suited us all. My mother and sisters, who had always been most comfortable in each other's company, had already become uncomfortable in mine. Lily only served to give their discomfort a focus, a subject upon which to seek solace and sympathy and become the centre of village talk for a while.

The villagers, as expected, had all seen Lily on her first day at one time or another – through a coffee shop window, from a passing bus, walking a dog past my mother's front door. It was not enough to be told about her – what she was wearing, how she did her hair – they had to see her for themselves. As for me, I gained more reflected attention through Lily than I had ever known from them before. Certainly, I had been admired – "He's a good-looking wee boy, your Harry" – but now I had risen to film-star status.

Yet, in a way, my life there had prepared me for a career in a large City firm, there were so many similarities – the gossiping, that was just as severe; the dramatic exchanges highlighted on e-mail distribution lists; the longing for information about a fellow employee that would be totally unknown by other members of the firm; the bitching; the calculated silences; the peering; the confidence derived from being part of a large group, which was so easily threatened by the presence of anyone different, daring, defying; the fear of the unknown outside world. No-one could have been more prepared for it than I was. And I did what I had taught myself to do over the first eighteen years of my life – I ignored it completely.

That was how I dealt with most aspects of life until I met Lily. Nothing really mattered to me then. I think that was why I was so successful professionally. Yes, I was a good lawyer, but there were many good lawyers. The difference between us was that I took chances. I gambled. I was prepared to take the consequences if things did not go according to plan. It was not that I could afford to be casual about my position. Unlike Lily, I did not have my own personal wealth to fall back on. But I had confidence in myself, and I was an optimist, and together those qualities carried me through my career with the fortitude of a row of twenty-ones on a black-jack table. If there was a tricky situation, it was given to Harry MacAllister to handle. If there was a difficult client, Harry MacAllister would sort him out. That was how it was. I played the hands I was dealt with the mastery of a magician, never dreaming that the day would come when I would unhesitatingly give up all I had achieved for the happiness of another.

14

I cannot explain why it came as such a surprise that I should be chosen. After all, Lily had singled me out; what greater achievement could there be than that? What higher accolade? Nothing in this world could have meant more to me. Her presence in my life was all I wanted.

Does that seem wrong? To place such high esteem on a mere mortal? More precious than my own soul, more precious than life itself, more precious than God?

There had been a time when nothing was as important to me as my belief in God. His existence had been as necessary, as indubitable as my own. As a child, I had visited Him in His church on the hill near our home. Every Sunday, He would open His doors for us and I would pour out my well-kept secrets. No-one else knew them. No-one else would have wanted to hear them. No-one else would have understood them. I longed for the preacher to say those words: "Let us pray," so that I could close my eyes and block out the rest of the world. I never listened to the names of those who were ill and in need of our prayers. I ignored the reverend's pleas for mankind, for the government, for the Queen, for the church, for dearly departed souls. They were not why I was there. To pray for them would have been as hypocritical as going to see Santa Claus to discuss what presents everyone else was getting. I was there for me. It was my time. No-one would spoil that for me.

It was not that our silent conversations were mundane or superficial. I did not list my selfish, childish needs and then wait impatiently for them to be met. That would not have been a conversation, and what I wanted more than anything else was to communicate. Communicate with someone who had the capacity and the inclination to comprehend. I did not want to be told that the reason why I was better at Maths than at Art was because I worked harder at Maths. That did not answer my 'why'. That did not offer me an explanation for why my brain worked in such a different way from James Donovan's, even though he and I were the same age, the same height and had always attended the same Maths and Art classes. Yet, when I asked God that question, He understood at once what I wanted to know, and suddenly my mind would be filled with a torrent of possibilities: genetic inheritance, childhood experiences, sociological influences, parental response, natural disposition, the individuality of each one of us in the midst of our extrinsic similarities. Of course, those were not the words I thought then as a child of eight or nine, but the impressions were there, as clear as day, and I would go from the church happily contemplating them to myself.

It was not until I was about sixteen that it occurred to me to doubt the existence of God. Surprising, really, when I had questioned so much else. I had read a book which had been given to me for French 'A' level. It was a well-crafted novel and the arguments were subtly interwoven with the plot in such a way that I began to have doubts about God's existence before I had even realised what was being questioned. Suddenly, I was left empty and numb, as if all oxygen had been sucked from my body. But, worst of all, the only Being to whom I could turn, to whom I had ever turned, was the very Being whose existence I now doubted.

Day after day, week after week, I sat alone – in a field, by the sea, at my desk – asking myself the same questions over and over again, creating arguments, finding counter-arguments, unable to reach any concrete conclusion but one : the only way to know for certain was to die. Before then, everything else was mere speculation.

Strangely, even then, the thought of death did not frighten me. Indeed, sometimes the idea was a welcome relief from the spiral of my thoughts. So that, when, on the day that I considered drowning myself in the sea, it was not so much the reaction of a fearful adolescent as the fearless response of an enquiring mind. What stopped me was the sudden realisation, as if I were back in the church on the hill, that if the answer were in the negative and there was no God, then I still would not know. I would be dead, and that would be the end of me, once and for all. As soon as my brain ceased to function, I would be unable to know either way. I would not just know nothing – for how can nothing be something you know – I would be nothing. More specifically, I would not be.

I stopped going to the church on the hill and I received a grade A for my French 'A' level. My parents never asked me why I no longer attended church with them on Sundays and I never told them. Over time, my belief in God came back to me, but never with the conviction I had once had. That kind of certainty was restricted to a belief in Lily. But the difference between my belief in Lily and my original belief in God was that Lily could let me down and I would still go on loving her, whereas if God let me down, that would give me reason to doubt his existence. How can an all-loving, all-powerful God let you down without creating a logical contradiction, after all? What I loved about Lily were not just her perfections, but her faults. But God was not allowed any faults without losing His identity in my mind.

Or so I thought. Until it happened. Before, that is, I was chosen, with Lily, to experience an event which would change our lives forever.

If only Lily could have believed in me as I believed in her. I wanted so much for her to trust me. If only she could have learnt to accept what I told her without requiring constant proof, then our life together would have been a happier one for both of us. But that was not Lily's way. She had an inclination towards disbelief just as I had an inclination towards Maths.

I could have refused Lily her proof, told her that it was up to her whether she believed me or not – but that would not have been fair. I had not always been truthful with Lily in the way that she wanted me to be, especially at the beginning of our relationship. And sometimes I found it difficult to understand exactly what it was that Lily wanted of me. What was I to tell her and what should be left unsaid? I do not wish to make excuses for myself – I know that I was responsible for exacerbating her tendency to distrust and I blame myself deeply for that – but Lily was always a difficult person to understand, and I had always found it hard to share my innermost thoughts. As a result, once Lily had found a reason not to trust me, the standard of proof she imposed became even higher until she could be certain that I would not let her down again.

Ironically, I knew how she felt. Not because I did not trust her, but because her response to me was the same as mine had been towards God. From the moment I had found reason to doubt Him, my standard of proof in His existence had come into play and escalated to a level which part of me realised would be impossible to achieve. If He let me down, He would not exist. If I let Lily down again, our love would have been a lie and I would cease to exist in her mind. On the other hand, no proof she could impose was sufficient to satisfy her uncertainties.

Just as I had contemplated death as a possible resolution, Lily had considered ending our relationship. For, if I were threatened with that finality, never to see her again, she would know from my response just how much she had meant to me. If I could not bear the thought of life without her, then surely I must have loved her. And I believe that the reason she never carried out her threats was much the same reason as mine for not throwing myself into the sea that day – if I did truly love her as she wanted to be loved, she would have terminated our relationship for nothing. And if I did not, she would not know anyway. So what was the point of the proof? What did it really show?

There were moments we shared when she would look at me as if she truly believed in me, and the world stood still: when we were running across a field, when we were swimming together in the moonlight, when I held her in my arms. Those were the times when proof was unnecessary. I know because those were the times when I did not need a proof of God's existence either. They were the clearest proofs that it is possible to achieve on this Earth. No skilfully constructed evidences can compare with those in persuasion.

But Lily was not me. Those times were not enough for her. She sought something else. She wanted the strength of my original conviction in God, untainted by doubt, pure, perfect, unchallenged. It was Lily who had shown me that that was not possible. She had taught me what it meant to have faith in someone else without requiring perfection, in spite of challenge, regardless of doubt, not by her example, but by the response she unwittingly drew out of me by the essence of her being. And I vowed that somehow I would teach her what she had taught me. "Prove it!" would be banished forever from her lips whilst I would continue, unrequested, to do just that.

15

I had read about our hotel in an article in the travel section of the Telegraph. "Paradise on Earth" was the heading which had attracted my attention. A photograph of the seventeenth century manor house hotel set in a valley of mountains and perched at the foot of the medieval village had me dialling reservations before I had time to show it to Lily. I booked the best suite in the hotel, which I hoped would be as exclusive as its prices suggested, and prayed that Lily would be happy with my choice.

It always took Lily longer than me to relax into a holiday. I was usually in high spirits by the time we arrived at the departure lounge of Heathrow airport. The idea of setting off for another country, entering into unknown territory where we could swim and explore and enjoy each other without the temporal constraints of an office and clients and cases to progress was enough to reduce me to an exuberant schoolboy again. What pleased me most was that I could be in Lily's company twenty-four hours of each day.

On that day – I think it was the fifteenth of October – Lily seemed more edgy than usual. I wondered whether I should have consulted her before booking the holiday. Perhaps she did not like the idea of going to Mallorca. Or maybe she was worried about her ears on take-off. The weather was not good – she had said she felt as if there was going to be a thunderstorm. She always knew.

"I'm so looking forward to arriving in all that sunshine. I looked up the temperatures and it is supposed to be in the eighties today," I said as we stared through sheets of rain waiting for our plane to arrive.

"We should have gone earlier in the year. September. You cannot rely on good weather in October," Lily replied, fingering the platinum and diamond cross around her neck which I had bought her one Christmas. I had chosen it myself without any help from Lily. I remembered trying to forget all about it as soon as I had bought it until Christmas Day, so that Lily would not guess what it was. It thrilled me to find that she had not. I put it on her that day and she had not taken it off since. I had noticed lately that whenever she was anxious or nervous she would run her fingers over its surface as she was doing now, sometimes moving the cross from side to side along the platinum chain. It was the third time she had done so that morning.

It was not until we were on the aeroplane that I realised that we had forgotten to call Mary. My concern for Lily's mood had made it slip my mind. But why had Lily forgotten to phone her mother? It was the first time I had known her to forget. She knew how much Mary worried whenever she was in an aeroplane. It was natural, since her father's crash.

I was about to ask Lily what was the matter when she suddenly turned to me as we were about to take off and kissed me on the cheek.

"What was that for?" I asked, surprised by her change of mood.

"Nothing in particular," she replied happily. I smiled at her, relieved that the thunderstorm had passed.

Almost as soon as we were in the air, Lily fell asleep. Her small face slipped comfortably onto my shoulder. I could hear her breathing become deeper and slower. I always knew when she was asleep. She became so still that it was as if she were in a coma, and she stayed that way until she began to dream.

It must have been a bad dream that day for I could hear her whimpering as she threw her head from side to side. At one point I thought I heard her say something, but I could not make out what it was. Then she was awake again as swiftly as she had fallen asleep.

She must have slept on and off for most of the flight. I endeavoured to stay awake, which was difficult as I had been working long hours for weeks before we had left London. I had been negotiating a multi-million pound settlement which was only completed six hours before our flight took off. At one stage, I had feared that I might not be able to get away in time. What would have happened then? Lily would probably have gone alone. Oh God! The idea of Lily enduring all that without me! No-one beside her to stroke her hair and kiss her forehead when it all began. No-one to protect her from the impact when our plane first collided with the runway, no-one to assure her that everything would be alright, that it was just a thunderstorm, that she should go back to sleep. No-one to cradle her in their arms and pray to God for her salvation.

Did she wake up? Did she know what was going on around her? Did she hear the screams of the women and children around us? Could she have looked so calm and peaceful if she had?

She opened her eyes just once for a second or two after we had crashed. I was barely conscious myself by then. But I never took my eyes off hers, until I could keep them open no longer. She spoke. It was almost a whisper.

"Can you hear anything?" she asked me.

"Only you," I replied through a smile. My last smile. My last words to her. Then all was darkness.

16

When I regained consciousness, she was gone. Someone must have moved us, for I was lying on a grassy slope several metres from the runway. I was on my back. When I opened my eyes, all I could see was a pale blue sky and sunlight. Strong, blinding sunlight. I tried to pull myself up so that I could look for her, but I was paralysed. I could only manage to move my head from side to side.

"Lily!" I cried out. "Are you there? Oh God, Lily, please answer me!" But there was no response. I knew there was a great deal of commotion somewhere in the distance, but somehow I was not aware of it. It was as if it were going on behind closed doors which I did not care to open.

I closed my eyes to save them from the sun's rays and to preserve what little strength I had left. I sensed a sharp pain in the centre of my chest whenever I inhaled, so I concentrated on keeping my breathing as shallow as possible and exhaling deeply. After a while – I have no idea how long – I heard a man's voice saying:

"Mr. MacAllister?" with a strong Spanish accent which conjured up an elderly man, but he was out of my limited line of vision.

I must have lost consciousness again. The next I remember is being driven uphill along a windy route through the Mallorcan countryside, and an aroma of pine trees wafting towards me through an open window.

I do not know whether it was the scent of pine trees that relaxed me or whether I had been given some form of sedative to ease my pain. But whatever it was, I felt a calm which I had not experienced before. It was almost as if I were in a transcendental state journeying through the clouds. Not fighting for my life, alone in a foreign country I did not know, desperate for knowledge of my wife who was no longer with me.

I must have fallen asleep about then, for I had a dream. It was unusual for me to remember my dreams. Unlike Lily who seemed to remember every one.

"You must have dreamt something!" she would tease me, "Everyone dreams – every night. Try and remember!"

"But there is nothing to remember. I did not dream anything."

"Then why were you talking in your sleep?" she would continue. It was difficult to dissuade Lily once she was on a certain train of thought.

"Was I? Again? Did it sound like me this time?"

"No. It was a deeper, faster voice than yours."

I had heard from her many times about my nocturnal alter ego but it did not concern me. Sleep to me was simply that. Nothing more, nothing less. The mind shutting down and unloading all the facts and impressions it had absorbed during the previous days, sometimes triggering former similar recollections and occasionally murmuring semi-recognisable gibberish in the early hours of the morning.

But to Lily, dreams were more than that. Dreams could foresee, warn, guide, if you knew what signs to look for. Dreams could take you onto a different plane where characters existed in their own right, independently of the being who came across them in their sleep. Dreams took those who knew how to look, to their guardian angels whose role was to guide their charge through difficult situations and point the way towards spiritual development. Dreams could take the dreamer back through a genetic myriad of layer after layer of ancestral memory to the source of a present anxiety. In short, dreams were not to be belied, and always to be remembered.

Perhaps there was a part of me which believed that too. Certainly, in Lily I had seen several examples of prophetic foresight through her dreams. I could not dispute that. But I preferred – most of the time – to put that down to her acute sensitivity with what went on around her. She read the signs that life showed her sometimes without even realising that she had done so until she fell asleep. Perhaps I was too afraid to accept any other explanation. It suited me not to dream – or not to remember my dreams. That way, there was nothing to interpret.

That day however was an exception. My dream was so vivid that I doubt I shall ever forget it. It began in a swimming pool which nestled into the surrounding mountains like a bird's nest in the branches of a tree. The water was cool and soothing on a hot day and its surface caught the sun's rays and teased them playfully. I was alone in the pool, swimming up and down, enjoying the views which each new length offered me. In the distance I could see an old, sleepy village with narrow roads that meandered up the hillside towards the church at the village's highest point. I wished that Lily was with me to admire it too.

As if my wish had been answered, she was there beside me. I picked her up in the water and swung her around and around in circles until we both collapsed, dizzy, into the pool's depths.

In an instant the scene had changed and we were sitting at a table on a terrace above the sea. It was evening now and we were dressed for dinner. I wore black tie and Lily was in a beautiful long lilac dress which I had never seen her wear before. We must have been dining alone – I did not notice anyone else around us. We were laughing and talking as I leant over the table towards Lily and said:

"I wish I could bottle this moment and keep it for ever."

Lily smiled and said:

"Perhaps you can."

At first we seemed happy. Blissfully so. I remember asking myself in the dream whether perhaps I was dreaming. I answered that I was not. The place was too real, Lily was too much like Lily and I was too aware of my experiences for them to be anything other than a reality. When I was swimming, I could feel the sun beating down on the top of my head, when I was dining on the terrace, I could taste the lobster, when I held Lily in my arms and we danced in the darkness of the evening, I could hear her breathing close to me. There was no quality present which I associated with dreaming, inexperienced as I was in that state. Nothing of the vagueness of fleeting moments that were lost almost as soon as they began, half images that confused identity into a melange of observations. All was there, neatly in place with a continuity that defied unreality. I knew that I was there, with Lily, as clearly and distinctly as I knew that my heart was beating faster and faster in my chest as I thought these thoughts and that something was terribly wrong.

When I realised in the dream that she had disappeared, I wished that I could wake up and find her lying peacefully next to me in our bed. Why had I chosen to hide behind that tree on the terrace just then, when we had been dancing so happily together? Had I thought it would amuse her? Had I hoped that she would find me there in a game of hide and seek that would lead to an intimate embrace? Could I not have waited a little longer for the security of our bedroom for that?

What tortured me most was remembering that she had called out to me: "Harry, don't be silly! Where are you?" And I, in my foolish hiding place, had remained silent, as if I had been struck dumb.

I combed the terrace over and over again. Suddenly, it seemed like daybreak. I could see more clearly where we were – or rather, where I was. A steep slope of green lawn led away from the terrace towards an area of arid land at its base. I followed its path, wondering all the while whether it had been Lily's too. The soil at the lowest point was hard like clay, in contrast to the moist, verdant grass which had led to it. It was the sort of inconsistency which dreams are made of, but, to me, then, it was a mystery which needed to be solved if I were ever to see my wife again.

I walked on, avoiding the cracks in the ground like a superstitious child, tiptoeing cautiously towards a dark, treeless mountain in the distance. She had come this way. I was certain of it.

I grew hot, my forehead burned, my feet ached, I sweated with anxiety. God knows how many times I called out her name into the muggy air in vain. Then I saw it – my hope, in the form of a small circle of lilac silk, lying incongruously upon the dehydrated soil like a flag. She had been there! I was approaching her! It would only be a matter of time!

17

My sleep must have been disturbed suddenly when they lifted me onto a stretcher. So vivid had been the dream that I was about to cry out:

"Lily! Are you there? I'm on my way to you! Hold on!"

I could still smell the pine trees, perhaps even more strongly than before. I was outside now. I could hear voices, urgent voices, talking to each other in Spanish.

"Aqui! Aqui!"

"Ha muerto?"

"Creo que no."

I knew enough Spanish to realise that I was dangerously close to death. But that did not concern me. What mattered was that I should find Lily. If she had died in the crash, I needed to know.

"Mi esposa. My wife. Lily."

I found it difficult to speak. My speech was slurred. It sounded like someone else I did not know.

Three sets of eyes were upon me in an instant as I lay on the stretcher, unable to move. The sun had disappeared behind a cloud, so I could see more clearly now. At first, I thought that they were three young women; their skin was so smooth and fresh, and their faces were rounded like children's, with large, gentle eyes that reminded me of Lily. Then one of them spoke. The first one, on my left.

"You must be patient, Mr. MacAllister." It was then I realised that I was looking at a man. He must have been in his mid-twenties, yet there was something about his presence which gave him an air of seniority beyond his years. It surprised me to find that he spoke without the trace of an accent. And yet his intonation suggested that English was not his native language. I was about to ask him where they were taking me when another voice said:

"We are nearly there."

The man in the centre spoke this time. He was taller than the first, with longer hair, which he pushed behind his ears as he spoke.

I felt the pain in my chest again, and there was a taste of blood in my mouth.

"Hold on!" said the first voice, whilst the man in the centre placed his hand on my chest on just the spot where the pain was coming from. Instantly, I was aware of heat exuding from his hand and into my chest. Then I felt a tingling sensation on the crown of my head. After that, the pain disappeared and the man withdrew his hand. I was about to thank him when the man on the far right, who had not yet spoken, said with a voice that was stern but reassuring:

"Look at me!"

As he spoke, the sky blazed with a light so strong that I was forced to close my eyes. When I opened them again, I could see him clearly. I had paid little attention to him until then. He was so far to the right that he had been almost out of my sight. Therefore, it was hard for me to do as he asked. I took a deep

114

breath, which was easy this time, and urged myself with all my strength to move.

Suddenly, I felt as if a heavy weight had been lifted from my body, like unblocking a dam. Life was flowing through my veins again, unrestricted, forceful, purposive. I sat up on the stretcher and looked hard at the man on the right for the first time. He was staring at me with a gaze so intense that I felt as if he were searching deep into my head to the place where my thoughts were kept. I noticed that he held his chin low, close to his chest, so that he needed to raise his gaze from under his eyebrows to meet mine. His eyes were not just intense, they were keen and intelligent. If I ever saw them again, they would be how I would recognise him. Who was he?

As if he had heard my unspoken question, the man in the centre said:

"That was Michael."

In the time that it took for me to turn my attention to the man in the centre and back to his right, Michael had gone, and a white vapour lingered in the air where he had been, like a cloud. I looked all around me, but there was no sign of him. Was it possible that I had imagined him?

"He comes and goes as he pleases."

Again, my thoughts had been answered before I had formulated them into words. It reminded me of being with Lily, knowing that she would guess what presents I had bought for her, or why I would be late back from the office, or who I had bumped into, before I had told her. But this man's gift seemed to be even greater than Lily's. I only had to begin to wonder, and my question was answered.

I was tempted to test him, so I wondered to myself what his

name was and waited for his reply. He did not answer, but instead looked at me with curiosity. I tried again. Still he remained silent, smiling at me now as if I had amused him. I grew impatient of my game and glanced away from him. What did it matter what his name was anyway?

"You know my name."

He was laughing as he broke his silence. It was an unusual laugh, which sounded from the depths of his chest and lit up his whole face with a level of vitality I had never seen before. Suddenly, I was laughing too. There was nothing else I could do, so contagious was it once it had begun. Then I found myself saying:

"Of course I know your name. It's Raphael!"

I must have looked surprised by my own words, for he said, tenderly:

"It's alright. I was just testing you, too!"

We had stopped laughing, as spontaneously as we had begun.

"Did I guess correctly?" I asked.

"It was not a guess. I let you know my name. And now that you know it, I hope you will use it. Often."

I liked Raphael. Lily would have liked him too, I thought, if only she were there.

"You know, you took away the pain in my chest with your hand. I can breathe normally again. That's a real gift you have, Raphael."

"I try to live up to my name," he replied with a smile. "Raphael means 'Healer of God'. Did you know that, Harry?"

"No, I didn't. But it doesn't surprise me. Nothing surprises me today. Not even that you know my name is Harry."

"Michael told me that."

"Michael? Your friend who comes and goes? How did he know my name?"

"Through Lily," was Raphael's reply.

18

It shocked me to hear my wife's name spoken by this stranger. I could hear my heart pounding in the chest which he had so recently healed. Now it felt as if it were about to explode.

"Raphael will answer your questions later, when we get there. For the time being, it is better for you to be calm and quiet."

It was the other man who spoke this time, still positioned on my left where he had remained throughout my conversation with Raphael.

"But, don't you understand? I have to find my wife. If your friend Michael knows where she is, then I must speak to him at once. Where has he gone?"

The two men helped me from the stretcher onto my feet. I was unsteady at first, and swayed from side to side like a drunk at closing time. They were shorter than me, my companions, although Raphael was taller than the other man. But they were strong, and with one on each side of me as I walked, I felt my confidence increase.

It was quiet now. The crowd I had heard from my stretcher had dispersed before I had been able to see them. I imagined that they had been taken to hospital where, no doubt, I was heading too. But had Lily been taken there already?

Half expecting an answer to my thought, I was disappointed

by the silence, and I knew then that I would have to wait. My questions would not be answered yet. My companions had made themselves understood. I was to do as I was told. There was no room for negotiation.

It seemed as if all my years as a tactical practitioner – taking the lead in cases, unwilling to disclose information to the other side until I was ready, smoothly promoting my own authority – had been reversed, and I was incapable of doing anything about it. Yet, strangest of all, I did not mind. In fact, I welcomed the role reversal, even though the information I suspected these men possessed was more important to me than anything else in the world. And, instead of analysing the situation, as was normally my way, I absorbed myself into it with the flexibility of some sort of Zen Buddhist.

That was how I felt, up there in the mountains with my two silent friends, physicians I supposed, breathing the clear, aromatic air and thinking of nothing other than the moment.

Before long I was noticing sounds I had not heard up till then: crickets whistling to each other, a ship's horn far below us at sea, a lemon falling from its tree onto hard ground, my own footsteps, which were so much louder than those of my companions.

It did not take me long to understand why we were continuing on foot for the rest of our journey. The route that we were obliged to follow had become so narrow that there would not have been enough room for the smallest of cars to pass. And, even if we had managed to drive through the tunnel of trees, our way would have been blocked by numerous branches, covering the ground like rustic confetti.

It struck me as a curious route to lead to a hospital, but I did not give it much reflection at the time. For some reason, I trusted these two men. After all, they had saved my life, hadn't they?

Presently, our path began to clear and widen, and I could see glimpses of sunlight through the trees. Ahead of us, a shaft of light cut across the forest and fell upon a building, which I had not noticed before. At first, I thought it was a mirage, so I tensed the muscles around my eyes in an attempt to see more clearly. The building remained constant, highlighted like an actor on the stage.

For a hospital, it looked warm and welcoming. Not the kind of institutional architecture to which I had become accustomed in England. This place could have been mistaken for a country house hotel. Its walls, which looked as if they had been mellowed by centuries of good living, were made of sandstone. Its windows, which were long and shuttered, lined three floors with seventeenth-century symmetry. Its chimneys, of which I counted five, carried heavily-scented clouds of smoke out towards the pine forests whence they originated.

As we drew nearer, I noticed that the building was encircled by a wide terrace which reminded me of my recent dream. Was it possible that Lily was right about dreams, after all? Had I foreseen this location on my way here in my sleep? Or had a part of me been here before?

"There is something familiar about the place. I feel as if I have been here before," I said aloud.

But the two men had gone. I was alone again.

I walked on excitedly. My heart was pounding once again, my newfound calm had deserted me. If this really were the terrace of my dream, where Lily and I had danced together in the moonlight, where I had hidden behind a tree, where Lily had disappeared and I, in my state of despair, had set out to find her, then she must have been here. Indeed, she may still be here, waiting anxiously for me to find her.

I stopped abruptly when I reached the terrace, and searched for clues. Uncertain what I was looking for, my eyes fell upon an oak tree growing on the terrace. It was a large tree, large enough to hide behind. I stared at the tree, fearful, expectant, half-dazed. Just then, a small black cat ran down the tree's trunk and walked serenely across my path, disappearing through an archway, which led to an inner courtyard.

I had never been a superstitious person, yet I found myself wondering if this might be a lucky omen. Lily would be certain of it. Encouraged, I walked hurriedly towards the entrance to the building.

A heavy panelled oak door, furnished with iron studs and a large handle, led into the reception area. On whitewashed walls hung textured abstract oil paintings, which complemented the building's blend of old and new, and gave a feeling of warmth to the room. Two panelled windows stretched from the beamed ceiling to the floor, their original shutters pinned back by hooks to reveal the beauty of the pine-covered mountains which I had only just left behind me.

At a desk in the corner of Reception sat a woman of about my age. When she saw me, she stood up and beckoned towards me with a long, red painted fingernail. The informality of the gesture took me by surprise, and I looked around me to see whether it had been meant for someone else, but the room was empty except for the woman and me.

When she walked towards me I noticed that she was wearing

121

a short black dress and patent black stiletto heels, which struck me as inappropriate in the mountains of Mallorca.

She did not stop walking until she was inches away from me, smiling suggestively all the while. I wondered whether to turn around and leave there and then, but my desire to find Lily was too great for that.

"I am looking for my wife!" I said in a tone which made the statement sound like an announcement.

The young woman shrugged and looked distractedly away.

"Have you seen her? Her name is Lily. She has thick blonde hair and a small face, with big blue eyes. She is very beautiful. You would not forget her."

The woman turned her gaze back towards me, but it was different now. Gone was the flirtatious smile and in its place was a look of venomous hostility. The transformation pleased me, and I went on:

"Do you understand what I am saying, woman?"

Her expression told me that she had of course understood. But had she seen Lily? When she turned around to walk back to her desk, I feared that I may have been too severe. I needed her help, after all. The two physicians who had brought me here had disappeared. This woman was my only chance, at least for the time being.

"Please help me!" There was no arrogance in my voice this time, only fear and humility. But it was not feigned in order to please her, to get her to help me. It was how I felt. Lonely and afraid, so very afraid.

"Follow me!" was all she said as she continued to walk in front of me without looking back.

19

I walked behind her down a long corridor. Occasionally one of her heels would catch between two of the ragstone tiles and she would lose her balance. Whenever that happened, I would stop abruptly in my tracks before she had time to fall back on me. After a while, she decided to take off her shoes altogether, and she swung them by their straps as she continued barefoot along the corridor.

We passed several closed doors on either side of us. There were slats in the centre of each one with writing on them, which I could not make out. It surprised me that we did not see anyone on our way, especially in view of the number of injured who must have been brought here after the crash.

The crash. It seemed a lifetime ago. But how long was it? I looked at my left wrist to where my watch should have been, but it was not there. It must have fallen off when I was dragged from the aeroplane. My wedding ring was still in its place on my left hand, though, just where Lily had placed it four years before. I had never taken it off and I never would. It was my only possession which I truly cherished. Symbols of wealth had never been important to me. It was symbols of love which mattered. The woman in front of me would not have understood that. Not in a million years. She would have looked at Lily in one of her beautiful dresses and resented her immediately for what she read as wealth bestowing on her such fortunate elegance. Little would she know that what mattered to Lily was the aesthetic quality of what she wore, the colour, the texture and, most important of all to Lily, the comfort. She was not a woman who wore her clothes like a public bank statement. She was just as happy in a little cotton night-dress. Her clothes were a part of her, to be looked after like friends, and kept clean just as they were when they were first created, pure, unblemished, but for no-one else's opinion but her own, and possibly mine.

My thoughts turned at once to our baggage, left far away, no doubt, in the midst of the debris which was once our means of transport: mangled iron, broken glass and a small heap of abandoned clothes on the runway. Lily's clothes, and mine, clinging to each other as we should have been now, if it had not happened. Perhaps we would have been sipping champagne somewhere on the island not far from where I now found myself. But it might not be too late. In moments, Lily and I could be reunited and the present would then be nothing more than a past nightmare from which we were suddenly woken.

The woman had stopped walking. She was speaking to some-one. It was a man. He seemed angry. Their voices were low. I could not hear what they were saying, even though I was standing just feet away from them. The man was shaking a finger at the woman, who was looking down at her bare feet. I noticed that even her toe nails were painted red, and she wore a gold bracelet around her ankle. The man was dressed in a white overall under which he wore a suit. He must have been a doctor, I remember thinking, relieved that at last there was someone other than the woman to help me find Lily. At first, he did not notice me. It was not until I spoke that he realised I was there.

"Excuse me," I interrupted as politely as possible. "My name is Harry MacAllister." I held out a hand, which he did not take. "I am looking for my wife, Lily. I believe she was brought here earlier today. We were in the crash at Palma Airport and got separated. She may have been looked after by one of your colleagues called Michael."

I could see the man clearly now. He was older than I had thought at first, which pleased me as it meant that he probably held a senior post. I paused, waiting for him to respond.

"Mr.…MacAllister?"

He frowned as he spoke, which made him look even older. Would he be capable of caring for my wife?

"Yes," I replied, "from London."

It occurred to me that he might not speak English as well as I had anticipated, so I continued more slowly than before:

"Our plane collided with the runway. I was brought here by three of your colleagues. One was called Michael, and the other Raphael. I was not told the name of the third."

"But I have no colleagues with those names."

He spoke with a strong Spanish accent, but he seemed to have understood what I was saying.

"Perhaps you know him as Miguel?" I asked, recollecting my schoolboy Spanish.

"Mr. MacAllister, as you can see, this is a small clinic, which I run, together with my staff. We are three physicians here and none of us is called Miguel or Michael or Raphael."

He was becoming irritated by our conversation, but he was professional enough to continue it:

"I heard that most of the injured men and women from the flight were taken to the main hospital in Palma. Have you spoken to anyone there?"

I was confused now. I had heard so many troubled voices from my stretcher. Why would they have been taken up into the mountains, only to be returned to Palma? And why had I been brought here myself? It did not make sense. I needed to think like a lawyer again:

"Do you have a list of all those patients who were admitted to your clinic today?" I asked.

"It would be a very small list, Mr. MacAllister," he laughed. "There was only one admission today. A young lady whose identity we have not yet traced. But she did not come from the crash, I am afraid."

He was running out of what little patience he had. My time with him was in danger of being terminated.

"May I see her? There is always a chance it may be my wife."

"She is very ill. Critical. I do not advise it."

My heart sank when he said 'critical', even though I doubted the young woman was Lily. But I forced myself to respond quickly:

"I did not catch your name?"

"Doctor Vio."

"Doctor Vio, I would be most grateful if you would let me see the young woman. If you have not identified her, then it is in your interests as well as mine that I confirm with you whether or not she is my wife, who at this moment, is a missing person."

I spoke with a tone that I reserved for tricky negotiations. It had never failed me before. Doctor Vio hesitated.

"Do you have any identification on you?"

I felt inside my inside pocket where I always kept my wallet, but it was empty.

"I must have lost my wallet in the crash," I said, surprised that I had not thought of looking for it sooner.

"Will you please take a seat in my consultation rooms?"

He held out a hand towards a room on my left and the woman opened the door for me. She had replaced her shoes while we were speaking and now she was pulling at the hem of her dress. This time, she did not attempt to look at me, but instead glanced nervously at the doctor, who said something to her in Spanish, which I did not understand.

She closed the door behind me and I was left alone in the room. It was a pleasant room, with French windows leading onto the terrace. I looked out at the mountains which had led me here. I had not realised just how high up we were. It must have taken hours for the driver to reach this point from Palma Airport.

As I surveyed the tranquil scenery from my lofty position by the doctor's windows, suddenly I began to feel dizzy. I longed for a cool drink of water. My strength, I feared, was waning. I had to keep going, for Lily's sake.

I caught sight of myself in a mirror over a large white fireplace stacked with dry logs in the corner of the room. My face was covered with lines of dirty, caked sweat, and my hair was greasy and unkempt. If it had not been for my drawn expression, I would have looked like a schoolboy caught wrangling with a classmate and taken to the headmaster's study.

Along my jaw line, there was a cut of about three inches in length, which had been bleeding but was now sealed with a hard dark crust. My recently dry-cleaned blazer, which I had carefully removed from its plastic covering the day before, was torn at the collar and splattered with a mixture of mud and blood.

What must the doctor have thought of me in this state? I could have been a drunk who had wandered into his hospital from the woods. Would I have trusted myself looking like this? I thought. He was probably on the phone to the local police station right now.

I wanted to leave at that moment. I wished myself running between the pine trees like a deer being stalked, catapulted through the forest by adrenalin, intoxicated by the excitement of living, fearful of death, conscious of my own fragile mortality, wondering which way to run to avoid the hunters, stumbling, picking up speed again, eager for an escape, a camouflage, an ally in the uneven contest. The arrows would pierce my flesh, but still I would carry on running. For as long as I kept going, I would still be alive. The moment my legs gave way, I would be dead. I would not feel the pain at first, my only means of measuring my defeat would be through my heartbeat. A little longer and I would be safe. They would not find me. I knew the woods better than they. It was my home, after all. It answered to my cry, it protected my mate, it fed me, it bathed me, and now it would hide me. And if I were hunted to death, I would die a glorious death in my home, I would die a deer's death amongst my own kind, not a mouldy, stagnant death, not a feeble, coward's death, not a hateful, spiteful, devious death, but the death of a free spirit, vital, energised, at one.

The door opened behind me. The doctor entered the room. He had removed his white overall. His suit was shiny with age. He sat down at his desk and lit a fat cigar, which he had taken from a drawer. The smoke polluted the fresh air in seconds. I turned my face back towards the open window and inhaled deeply, half expecting the pain in my chest to have returned, but it had not.

"You were on the 10 a.m. flight from London Heathrow to Palma. You sat over the wing with your wife. You only had hand luggage with you. Is that correct?"

So he had telephoned the airline, not the police.

"You know it is," I replied sternly. "Now what?"

"Your wife was not identified amongst the survivors. She is not at the hospital in Palma."

He puffed at his cigar until he was satisfied that his mouth was sufficiently full to exhale.

"I am afraid, Mr. MacAllister, that it looks as if your wife is dead."

His face was blurred through the smoky veil that enveloped him like a dark aura. He had placed an arrow in his bow and aimed it at my chest. I did not feel any pain. My body was numb.

"You are making a huge assumption, Doctor Vio. A scientific induction from very shaky premises. But then, you are a scientist, and that is what scientists do. Whereas, I am a lawyer, and lawyers prefer facts. Now, will you take me to the patient who was brought in today, or do I have to go to the police for assistance?"

Doctor Vio pressed the lit end of his cigar into an ashtray until it was extinguished. The air began to clear and I could see him again. He stood up and headed towards the door, gesturing for me to follow him.

"Expect to be disappointed," he said gruffly.

"How can you be certain that she was not from the crash? You said she was unconscious, did someone bring her here?"

My thoughts turned to Michael again. Could it be possible that he had left her at the clinic without saying who either of them was? Raphael had told me that he came and went as he pleased. And, if Lily had truly told him my name, then she must have been conscious at some stage in his presence.

The doctor continued to walk ahead of me along the corridor as he spoke:

"I found her myself in the woods earlier today. She was lying in a clearing at the foot of the pine forest below the clinic. I saw something from the terrace outside my window. I often stand there and look out at the trees. It relaxes me to observe them, when I am surrounded in here by so much sickness and misery."

For a second, I glimpsed a different Doctor Vio. Was it possible that I had misjudged the man?

"When I first approached her, I thought I was looking at a dead animal. There are sometimes deer stalkers in the forest; we find deer carcasses at the entrance to our grounds. They must head to us hoping for protection, I suppose. Somewhere they can hide in safety from their hunters. But by the time they reach here, it is often too late for them."

He was speaking in a whisper now, which I found difficult to hear. So I walked a little faster until I was alongside him.

"When I drew closer and realised that it was in fact a young woman, I thought that she was sleeping. She looked so calm and peaceful, as if she were in the middle of a pleasant dream. But there was no pulse. Her heart had stopped beating."

He cupped both his hands over the area of his chest that housed his heart, in a gesture of illustration.

"It took a great deal of effort to get it started again," he added proudly. "I have a good team here, but we do not normally admit patients who are so severely ill. We do not have the equipment here, you see. We are a small, private clinic, specialising in holistic care. But in an emergency, you have to do what you can."

I thought he had finished speaking when he continued:

"It mystifies me, I have to say. She has not regained consciousness, although there are no obvious signs of injury or disease."

20

The room where they had taken her, the woman with no identity, was on the first floor at the front of the building. There were no lifts in the clinic, so the doctor and I had to climb a wide, carved oak staircase that smelled of wax polish.

When we reached the first floor, the doctor paused, out of breath, and I wondered how he managed to cope with the physical constraints of his profession. He must have seen me looking at him, for he said:

"It is a very hot day today. Humid. No air."

There was a wide landing with four doors leading off it, two on either side of us, and a double sash window straight ahead. On the walls hung large, brightly-coloured oil paintings, which I imagined must have lifted the spirits of many patients.

"They are all painted by local artists," the doctor said proudly.

We approached a room numbered 12 on the door. My pulse raced. I could feel my legs begin to give way. The doctor grabbed my arm just as I was about to fall, and led me to a long narrow bench against a wall, under a painting of the Queen of Diamonds. He laid me down on my back and raised my knees to my chest. Then he listened to my heartbeat. I felt a fool, a weak, incompetent idiot in the hands of a man whom I had been trying so desperately to outwit.

To my surprise, Doctor Vio seemed genuinely concerned for my well-being, and the more grateful I appeared, the more he tried to help me. In seconds, he had flung open door 12 and returned with a jug of cold water and a glass.

"Sip this slowly," he said, pouring the liquid into my mouth while he held me up with his left arm.

"You are trying to do too much. Relax here a while. Have you eaten today?"

I shook my head. He returned with a big bowl of fruit; oranges, bananas, pears, plums, grapes.

"Try the grapes. They are very sweet," he said, as he placed one between my lips. I swallowed it whole, and thought it was the most succulent grape I had ever tasted.

He sat at my feet and took off my shoes and socks. Then he massaged scented oil between my toes in circular movements. It was a wonderful sensation. I felt as if the tension was disappearing out of the soles of my feet.

"Thank you," I said quietly, but he was not listening to me. So I added, as if to share something with him in order to repay his kindness, "She cannot be dead, you know, because she has spoken to Michael about me. Raphael told me. They knew where she was, I could tell."

The doctor nodded as if he were listening to the ramblings of a delirious man. After that, I fell asleep.

Strangely, I did not dream of Lily this time, but of her mother, Mary. She was wearing a long black dress with a train that brushed the ground as she walked, and in her hand she was carrying a white lily.

She seemed surprised to see me, and looked at me as if she had seen a ghost. I was about to speak to her when she raised her finger to her lips in a gesture of silence. I obeyed, and followed her path, curious to know where it was leading. Presently, we came to a lake set amidst rolling lawns of green, dotted here and there with colourful wild flowers. Sunlight was shining on the scene, giving it a warm glow reminiscent of lazy summer days in England.

There was a swan floating on the surface of the lake with her young following behind her in a line. The length of her white neck coupled with her upright bearing added to the dignity of her appearance, as she sailed past me like a mighty yacht.

By the side of the lake there was a willow tree, with branches that drooped into the water like Rapunzel's hair. Mary pointed towards the tree as if she wanted to show me something. I scanned the area all around it, but could see nothing that might be of relevance to Mary or to me. Mary grew agitated. I looked again. This time, I saw something. A shape at first. Nothing more than that. Then, as I focused harder, I saw the shape move. It was coming towards us. Mary smiled at me, and waved at the figure approaching us. I could see now that it was a woman. I hoped she would be wearing a lilac dress, but she was not. I longed for her to have thick, long blonde hair, but she did not. This woman had short brown hair, which looked as if she had taken a pair of scissors to it and hacked it off. She smiled back at Mary as if she knew her, but there was something about her demeanour which suggested that she would rather not be smiling, that it troubled her to do so, that she had no right to be happy.

Mary went to meet her, but I stayed where I was. If Mary wanted me to follow her, then she would let me know, just like the swan with its young. When she reached the woman, she handed her the white lily she was carrying, and folded the young woman's hands gently around it as if it were in danger of crumbling.

The young woman looked down at the flower in her cupped hands and began to cry. Her tears fell from her eyes in streams, which followed the contours of her face and then came to rest on the pure white petals of the lily, like dewdrops.

When I woke from the dream, the doctor was gone. He had covered my body in a white linen sheet before he left, and the water jug was full again. The landing was perfumed with the aroma of the scented oil which he had rubbed into my feet. The smell of it reminded me of the wild flowers growing by the lake in my dream.

I should have thought of Mary before. She had a right to know what had happened to us, to me – and to Lily. But, what could I tell her? That I was safe, but her daughter…what? Missing? Believed dead? It would not be the first time that Mary had been the recipient of such news. And an air crash again. How could she cope?

I pictured her sitting alone in her home in the countryside, her haven she called it, listening to the news, waiting for Lily to phone, not daring to go out in case she missed her call. When she heard nothing from us, she would have contacted the airport and our hotel. Would they have known what had happened? Would she already have been told? I should be the one to break the news, not some stranger at the end of a telephone. It was my duty.

I stared at the door in front of me. Number 12. Is that a lucky number, my Lily? You were always drawn to palindromic numbers. If it had been you, they would surely have put you next door in room 11, without even knowing why. Just like when we found our flat in South Kensington, number 44, and we were given our new telephone number 3113, and we bought our first car together CBR 606. It could not be you on the other side of door 12.

I pulled myself unsteadily to my feet. Lily did not deserve a coward. I had to find out. I could see the end of the bed through the partially open door. It was a large white king-sized bed with hand-carved barley twisted oak posts at the two corners. I took a step closer. Two long French windows led onto an ornate iron balcony beside the bed, to the left as I looked into the room. Straight ahead of me there was another set of French windows with shutters that were closed. That was all I could see without pushing open the door and entering the room.

I did not need to hesitate. The decision was made for me. The door was opened from inside.

"I knew you would come," said a voice I recognised.

21

I was happy to see him again. It felt like meeting an old friend, even though we had only spent minutes together. And he greeted me as if I were his friend, too.

"That is because you are," said Raphael, placing his hand on my shoulder. Instantly, my spirits soared and my body felt stronger.

"Doctor Vio said he had not heard of you," I spoke in a whisper as Raphael had done.

"He does not know I am here. Only you have seen me. But I told you I would answer your questions when we got here, didn't I? So here I am!"

I did not take my eyes from his as he spoke, not because it mattered to me, at that moment, why it was that Doctor Vio did not know who Raphael was, but because I did not dare to allow my gaze to rest upon the bed.

"Now ask me what you want to know."

I had only one question on my mind at that moment, but it was one I dared not ask. Surely he realised that? He had read my mind before.

"You want to know," he continued, "whether it is your wife who is lying unconscious in the bed."

I nodded my silent confirmation, fearful that a tear would

destroy the impression I had been working so hard to achieve since I had arrived there.

Raphael looked hard into my eyes, just as he had before, by the roadside, only for longer this time. What could he see of me? I wondered. Things that I could not? Potentials not yet achieved? Fears not yet conquered? Strengths not yet recognised? Tests not yet addressed?

Finally he said, quietly closing door 12 behind him:

"You are not ready. This is not the time. Come!"

And he ran down the stairs, like a child, eager to show his toys to his new friend. At the foot of the staircase, there was a small door, which I had not noticed when I was with Doctor Vio. Raphael pushed hard against it with his left shoulder, but it would not open.

"Let me!" I said, noticing for the first time how small his frame was. From where I stood behind him, he could have been mistaken for a woman, with his long, fair hair and slender back, and dressed in a full, coral-coloured coat that reached to the ground.

I took hold of an iron door handle and pushed. To my surprise, the door opened easily.

"After you!" I said confidently, happy that for once it was I who had been able to offer some assistance rather than he. Raphael hurried through the opening and along a narrow footpath, overhung with flowers of every colour of the rainbow. The Mallorcan sun was at its mellowest now, casting a golden glow upon whatever it touched. In the distance, Raphael looked as if he had bathed in a stream of liquid gold, and the clinic's walls were the colour of yellow amber.

Neither of us spoke as we embarked upon a sharp ascent,

which took us past crooked old trees, heavy with ripe black olives. Such was the incline that by the time we reached the top, we could see over the roof of the building to the mountains beyond. It was a heavenly view. How I wished that Lily were there to see it with me.

I wanted to throw myself to my knees and lift my head to the sky and pray to God there and then for her safety. Would He listen? Had I been absent from Him for too long?

"God always listens," said Raphael softly, "But, do you?"

I thought about the question for a moment, and then answered:

"I try, but sometimes I cannot hear anything. I used to, when I was a child. I would go every week to church then. It was a beautiful church, high up on a hill a little like this one. I had so many questions for Him and I thought I heard His answers. But then…"

I wanted to tell him about my doubts, that had tormented my teenage years, but I could not.

"Then I stopped."

"Stopped what? Listening or believing?"

"Both," I replied.

"Then why don't you try again?"

I focused on the highest peak of the mountain ahead of us. It was a dark mountain, unlike the others around it. No pine trees grew on this mountain. Indeed, as far as I could see, no vegetation grew on it at all. It stood like a giant volcano, devoid of a living spark. As I stared silently ahead of me, I emptied my head of every thought, as if I were back in the church on the hill, and looking at the altar.

Then I listened. I was a child again, believing totally,

unconditionally in a God I could not see, assuming without question that He would answer me. I closed my eyes, just as I used to do, and concentrated hard on the darkness inside my head.

That was when I saw her, Lily, walking down the side of the dark mountain I had only just shut out. She was dressed in lilac, just as she had appeared in my dream, only the dress was shorter and looked as if the hem was uneven. She seemed happy, she was smiling her sweet, gentle smile. Her mass of long hair was blowing behind her in the breeze, like a mane. She was speaking. There was someone with her. It was a man. A white vapour lingered in the air around him, like a cloud.

I opened my eyes with a start, and said:

"It is Lily in the bed, isn't it?"

"Yes," came the reply.

Part Three

EVE

22

No-one knows my story. How could they? No-one was there. Except Adam. And he shared but a part of my life. It carried on without him, when he was gone, and I was left to live out the role that God had begun for me. Was that His plan too? That I should decide to remain here, in this impasse of despair?

Certainly, it feels like a decision, when I search inside the silence of my mind for an answer, alone with no-one to influence me this time. It seems as if I am in control of the pattern of my thoughts. But how can I be sure? I may be nothing more than an actor on His stage, thinking the thoughts He writes for me, performing His scenes to the applause of an audience of His angels.

I played my part well, though, didn't I? Surely, that was my own individual stamp – the quality of my performance, even if I am no more than that.

Adam thought he understood: God had created us, Adam first, and then me as his companion, his helper. I was to be inferior to him, but Adam would not accept that. He needed me, he said. His life would be incomplete without me. He would rather die with me than live without me. Or so he thought, little knowing then what death entailed.

I still believe my husband was my superior. He was stronger, braver, purer than his wife. He believed what God told him without question. His faith endured when mine began to sway.

"We are his chosen two, Eve," he would say, "God loves us so much that He has given us all this to enjoy."

And how we enjoyed it then, in the beginning! Like two innocent children experiencing the miracles of life for the first time. How I have longed for just one moment more of that time we shared together before it happened. To see the morning sun shining on mellow fields, verdant pastures. To smell the nectar as it fed each plant and flowed into flower after flower of His Creation. To hear the gentle murmur of rippling waters falling down the hillside to a tranquil resting place in the lake below. To breathe the aroma of healing herbs that purify the senses with their magic powers. To taste ambrosial fruits, plucked from laden trees (ah, what double-edged joy!) To sit in shady groves and listen to a happy chorus of birds singing their songs of freedom with outstretched wings. And docile, fluffy flocks of sheep, grazing with a watchful eye upon their frolicking young, those timid creatures but with such capacity for joy! But, above all, to know that my beloved Adam was never far away from me.

Together we tended the flowers that grew wild in our garden, and talked to the animals who sought us out, captivated by our presence as we were by theirs. When we grew hot from a day's labour in the fields, we enjoyed the cool lake's water even more, never once dissatisfied with our lot. Work was not a burden when it was shared by us. Everything we did together was a joy, a moment to savour, cherish for eternity, or so we believed then. Ours was a world free of guile, free from secrets, from animosity or jealousy. Each new day brought with it a new

144

experience: the discovery of a plant we had not noticed before, the approach of a timid animal who had learnt at last to trust us, the beauty of a rainbow arched over our Paradise like an angel's wing.

And we shared it all with a grateful heart and an unquestioning trust in God's grace. We were His chosen two. What greater proof of His love could there be? Yet our lofty position did not go to our heads. We were just two innocent, trusting lovers, grateful for the honour that had been bestowed upon us, as pure in thought as in deed, as gentle towards our environment and every creature within it as we were towards each other. The perfect couple for a perfect environment. Was that His plan? Did we play our parts well?

I can ask that now because now I know what it is to be tormented by doubts and disbelief. I am innocent no longer. Like a garment of pure silk that has been torn in half, I shall never be what I once was. The tear will always be visible. I am imperfect.

I never meant to hurt him. He was everything to me. Even our banishment I could endure happily so long as he was with me. He did not deserve to be punished. It was I who did wrong. I should have been exiled alone.

"But that would have been a greater punishment for me," he told me, "to continue living in Eden without you, surrounded by memories of you everywhere I looked, but no longer able to take joy from them. You made it Paradise, Eve. Without you, it would soon have turned to Hell."

So his fate was inevitable once I had done wrong. I caused his downfall. I brought about his suffering.

He tried to tell me it was not my fault, I had been the victim of evil. Evil fed on goodness, he said. It made victory taste even better.

But I did not accept that. I had been given a choice. I had free will. God had created us that way so that there would be true virtue in our good deeds. Adam had explained it to me many times, and I believed what he told me then, like a child.

But, like a child also, I became curious. If God had given me free will, a capacity for choice, then why had he imposed a restriction on me without giving me a reason? "Keep out!" no more tests moral value than it proves the motives of the trespasser. And so I trespassed.

23

I have replayed those early days so often in my head, as if I hoped that, somehow, in so doing, I could erase what had been done and reshape what has long since gone. It is a failing of mine, an inability to accept what is lost: there must be something I have missed, if I can only find that missing piece, everything will fall into place. The "Whys" will become "Becauses" and I shall move on. But the search is in vain. There is nothing more I can add to the story of my life. I know it all, every detail, every word, every look, every question, every deed, every wrong. Nothing new can change it, that is why I am here, locked in this purgatory, my self-inflicted punishment – the exile I should have been given by God, alone, without Adam, without my children. It is the only choice I can feel certain is my own. God would not have chosen this path for me, would He? There is no purpose for Him in a status quo. His way is solutions, mine is stand-still.

Does He think I do not sense Him watching me, fearing for my salvation? Does He believe I have been punished enough? His decision, not mine. I am prepared to remain in this state for eternity. I deserve nothing else. That is my decision.

So He sends Michael to me, dear, sweet Michael, the saviour of our souls, the heavenly advocate on behalf of earthly mortals.

I have seen him with others, I saw him with my own sons. What tears he weeps when he fails in his godly duty! It moved me at first to witness a being as manly as Michael, strong and brave like my Adam, crying like a baby for lost souls. But he does not cry for mine. He thinks he can succeed, that it is only a matter of time.

And now they have sent the woman with the flaxen hair. Lily. They think she will persuade me with her female argument – a fellow inferior who will understand me, who will speak my language.

Michael told me that she was an advocate. He would like that. It would give them something in common. I have noticed a bond between them. She knew him before she came here I am certain. Perhaps that is why she became a barrister on earth, because he chose her career without her even being aware of it. He is subtle in his persuasion. It would not have been difficult for him to plant a few seeds in her subconscious while she slept, unaware of his presence, or in a conversation when he looked deep into her innermost thoughts. And now she thinks it was all her decision, poor creature!

Yet, I like her. There is something about her which reminds me of what I once was, before it happened. She is curious, she wants to understand. I can see that in her keen, lively eyes and her open smile. She wants me to trust her, she is willing me to allow her to help me, not for her sake but for mine, but, like me, she is afraid. Of what I am not sure, but I shall find out. Because I want to help her too. She thinks she does not need help, but she does. She thinks she is here for my sake, but she is not. She thinks He sent her to me to fight for my soul, but she is wrong. Or perhaps she is half right. I believe He sent her to me because

He knew that I could save her too. And I shall. I did not understand that until now, this instant. It may be that I did not create the thought by myself at all. Who knows? But it is mine now. I have heard it. I alone am responsible for that. And I shall act upon it. I shall let the girl think that she is helping me and I shall listen. I am good at that. Eventually it will become clear to me what it is she fears.

It was Michael who first told me she was coming. I remember, I was sitting reading the blind poet's book. Was that vain of me? Not really (and defy those fools who say "Not really" really does mean "Yes"). He possessed a deep insight that man. He must have had a vision without sight. Strange how closer we move to the very thing we lose.

"There is someone I would like you to meet," Michael said to me. I put down my book and looked up to where he towered over me.

"Who is it?" I asked, somewhat surprised. He had never introduced me to anyone before. I thought he understood that I wanted to be alone. I did not deserve the company of others. I was to blame for their suffering after all. Wasn't that what everyone said? Eve, first created woman, tempted by a serpent to eat the forbidden fruit and bring the taste of death and shame and guilt and pain to all mankind. Who would want to meet me?

Michael did not reply at first. I think he was listening to his Master. I did not ask again. I understood Michael. He would tell me only what he thought I should know.

"Will you speak to her?" he asked.

"Do I have a choice?" I replied, laughing at the question that seemed to torment my every thought.

"Of course you do, Eve!" He chastised me with a sidelong glance as he sat down beside me. That was when I realised that this was a matter of great importance.

"She is alone here, too." He treaded cautiously.

"What! No husband either!" I asked with an air of sarcasm which I knew at once did not suit me.

"Not here," was all that Michael would say.

I did not know what my response should be, so I said nothing.

"Thank you," Michael said, then left.

I picked up my book and continued to read, when suddenly he was back again beside me.

"Why does it have to be like this, Eve?" he asked in a whisper as he stared ahead of him.

"You know why. We have been through it all before. Ask your Master. It was His plan."

"You do not really believe that. He only wants what is best for you….. and Adam."

As soon as he said my husband's name, he realised he had gone too far. But it was too late.

"Are you trying to hurt me more than I hurt already?" I said angrily. Michael shook his head.

"Then why do you mention his name?"

He had no answer.

"We are no longer a pair. He is gone. There is no Adam and Eve any more. There is only Eve. Please do not forget that again!"

Michael buried his head in his hands. He had not meant to cause me pain, I knew that, just as I knew that I was being too harsh on him. But I could not control my temper whenever certain subjects were brought to the surface, however hard I tried. It was like trying to bury a volcano. Better to let it erupt and wait until the lava had cooled down.

"I am sorry, Eve," Michael lowered himself onto one knee as he spoke and stooped his head. I laid my hand on his shoulder in a gesture of reconciliation.

That was when she saw us – Lily, the girl. I sensed her hesitation, but I did not stir. Neither did Michael. He wanted to ensure he was forgiven before he moved.

The first thing I noticed about her was a small cross which she wore around her neck. I watched how she moved it from side to side on its chain as she stood silently, shyly, respectful of our privacy. I remembered how it felt to be self-conscious, suddenly aware of one's own identity and embarrassed by it.

It hit me like a thunderbolt when it first happened to me. Before then, I had been no more aware of my own body than I had of Adam's or any creature around us. It had never occurred to either of us to hide ourselves in clothing to shield any embarrassment we might have felt at ourselves, no more than I would have clothed a lion or its mate. Together we were one then, particles of the whole, separate but joined by a living force, an energy that ran through us all – the birds, the lions, the sheep, the lake, the mountains, the gardens, the sky, the earth, the plants, the trees and each other. We had all been created by the same Maker, each of us had a vital role to play in our mutual existence. I, Eve, was not important as a single entity. I needed every other aspect of our life for my survival, just as the plants and trees needed me. I possessed no ego. I had no goals. I barely questioned who I was. And if Adam did matter more to me than the plants I watered, or the trees whose fruit I plucked, then that was because Nature had pronounced it to be so in order that we might procreate and continue what He had begun.

But all that changed. I made a mistake. I sinned. There is no point in denying it or trying to mitigate the damage that I caused. And from that moment, everything around me changed. I felt emotions I had not experienced until then – shame, embarrassment, fear, anger, guilt and much more. I saw my world as I had not seen it before. Birdsong made me weep, trees and their fruit made me shake with anger, Adam's goodness stung me with remorse. I looked down at my naked body and saw it with eyes which were no longer innocent. I was tarnished. I would never be the same again. Suddenly I understood what it was to have a personal identity, and I wished I could be anyone other than Eve.

Eve became the focus of my every attention. Eve was to blame for everything unpleasant and undesirable. Eve had allowed pollution to enter our pure hearts. Eve had let herself be led astray – and oh so easily – Eve had been tested and had failed. So crammed was my head with every conceivable negative thought that I overlooked the beauty of the world around me. The sun no longer shone for me, the flowers were too bright, their scent displeased me, the playfulness of creatures around me only served to remind me of my own lost innocence. But, worst of all, was the look of disappointment on Adam's face. At first, I hid from him ashamed to be near him. But he always found me, as if he knew instinctively where I would be.

But that part of my tale is too painful to tell, although I remember it well. Perhaps somewhere Adam is recalling it too, perhaps he no longer needs to, perhaps he is the lucky one, after all. I never ask about him now. I am too afraid, like the girl, Lily, although the difference between us is that I know what I fear.

That cross must be important to her, she fingers it like a crutch. Yet she does not strike me as a religious person. She is too troubled, too uncertain, like me. It was probably a present from someone she loved – loves. Michael said she has no husband here – she must have left him behind, or perhaps he left her. She is loved. Of that I am certain. She carries herself like someone who is cherished, as if she is holding a precious stone in the palm of her hand, anxious not to let it fall, proud to have been entrusted with it all the same. But she fears it will be stolen from her grasp when she is not looking. So she fastens her fist a little tighter, hoping that the gem will not be seen, until it cuts hard into her fragile fingers and she lets it fall.

24

M ichael was the first to speak.
"Lily, come and meet Eve!" he said, raising himself
from his stooped position at my feet.

She took a step towards us, still hesitant. Suddenly I was
filled with a desire to reassure her. I wanted to tell her that I
understood how it felt to be uncomfortable with one's own
presence.

"Lily. What a beautiful name! Like the flower."

I heard my words, but I barely recognised the speaker. It was
as if I had been transported back to a time when God's creation
was a wondrous thing to me. My anger had gone. I yearned for
an opportunity to share a long-lost side of me with this stranger.

I noticed her looking at the cover of the book I was reading –
Paradise Lost. I had read it over and over again as if it contained
a key to my existence, if only I could find it.

"Have you read it?" I asked, although I knew from her
expression that she had. At least she would understand something of me already.

"Did you enjoy it?" I went on, urgently seeking out confirmation of her approval.

I should have anticipated that the question would lead to
an answer which referred to Adam. How could anyone read

Milton's poem without thinking of us both? I flinched when she mentioned his name. She saw me, but pretended not to notice. I liked her all the more for that, especially in the light of Michael's clumsiness moments before.

Poor Michael! I do not wish to sound ungrateful – he has been a true friend to me, my only friend, until Lily. But sometimes he can be too direct. I suppose it is a by-product of his telepathic abilities. He answers questions too quickly, before they are verbalised, while they are still in embryo in the thinker's mind. Occasionally, they would never have been asked at all, but would have drifted off into the person's subconscious and been reformulated into a totally different question, or even an answer. But Michael's mercurial interceptions prevent that from happening naturally. "Back off!" I want to say to him sometimes. "Give me some time!" But time is a concept which Michael has difficulty comprehending. It does not exist for him as we know it, Lily and I. He has no past, no present, no future. Everything he is exists now, has always existed and always will, spread out like an intricately woven carpet with no beginning or end. We find it hard to comprehend, we who are so blighted by the guilt of our past actions that we ignore the present and fear for the future. We cannot reduce a mind like Michael's to markings on a page. If we try, our words restrict us to the sum of our very limited experiences.

She would know what I mean – Lily. She sees it in Michael as I do. His answers do not surprise her, though – she seems to expect them, even if she does not always understand what he says.

"Don't you know yet, Lily?" he replied to her silent question.

155

"You are in Purgatory – suspended between two states of existence, waiting until it is decided where you will go next – you and Eve."

She took the news well. Not like me. I could not bear to be reminded. So I cried like a silly child. Until she threw her arms around me and said:

"There is no need for you to be afraid any more, Eve. I am here to help you."

Did all my years of existence count for nothing before this young woman? Had I acquired none of the wisdom that age is said to bring? Compared with me, she could have experienced nothing of the world; crumbs from the table of my life, at most. What suffering of hers could come close to mine? Yet there she sat, like a sage, wiping away my childish tears and comforting me with her understanding. God had not just sent his favourite angel to me this time, he had sent a mortal, someone who knew what it was to sin, to make mistakes and to curse oneself for them. What could Michael know of that?

It was not a question that he could answer, for he had gone. I never asked where he went when he disappeared. It did not matter to me. I knew he would return.

Lily looked anxious when she noticed that he was not there, as if her safety-net had been removed. It must have taken years for her to reach that stage of reliance – probably, she had known him ever since she was a child.

"He comes and goes as he pleases," I said to her. "There is nothing anyone can do to prevent that."

She seemed not to hear my words, or if she did, they were irrelevant to her thoughts at that time. So was I. She needed time alone to reflect. But where could I go? I never left this place, I did not permit myself the possibility. It occurred to me to hide behind a tree. Does that sound foolish, like some children's game of hide and seek? It was all I could think of at that moment. Lily would look around her and assume that I had followed after Michael, wherever it was that he had gone.

I was about to run and hide when suddenly Lily took the book from my hands, saying as she did:

"Which part are you reading?"

I was taken aback for a moment by her new-found confidence and did not reply. Instead, I pointed to the paragraph which I had been reading before she arrived. They were favourite lines of mine. When I read them, quietly, I pictured myself with Adam again, fearing for our future, tortured by our past mistakes, my mistakes, desolate at the prospect of leaving our beloved home. Milton was correct in his imaginings – it took Michael to remind me of what really mattered at that time. Not soil, not environment, not moments we had already lost. I could live without any of that. What was important to me was that my husband was by my side. The rest was replaceable. My husband's love was not:

"Lament not Eve, but patiently resign
What justly thou hast lost, nor set thy heart
Thus overfond, on that which is not thine.
Thy going is not lonely; with thee goes
Thy husband; him to follow thou art bound;
Where he abides, think there thy native soil."

How well Michael knew us both then, Adam and me. He was almost like our spiritual brother, guiding us through the most difficult parts of our life together. Did he love Adam more than he loved me? Perhaps. I never enquired. But those words of his, captured so well by the poet, make me think that he loved us both equally, and that pleases me in the midst of my despair. So I think on them and try to recapture time. Of course, I know that I try in vain, but, what matter? The trying brings me closer anyway.

It lifted my spirits to hear the girl read the lines that I had only ever heard silently inside my own head. And she read them so well, as if I were speaking them myself.

"You understand!" I cried, beaming with contentment. I wanted to throw my arms around her as she had done with me moments before, and tell her everything. Things that no-one else could guess, not even the poet. But, would she understand that too?

Just as I was wondering whether to tell her more, she said:

"The person addressing you in those lines was clearly very close to you. Who was it?"

I hesitated. I had to make a decision. Could I trust her? Before I had time to decide, Michael decided for me:

"It was I," he said, before he disappeared again from view.

She put down the book and gazed abstractedly around her. The moment was gone. I got up and ran towards a willow tree, which was a favourite of Michael's. Its branches hung low to the ground like the long, flowing hair which once had served to cover me so well. It was a perfect hiding place. I heard her call my name, but I did not respond. Then she called out for Michael, half-heartedly this time. I peeped between branches as I pushed them aside, and saw her sitting in the same spot, downcast, desolate. Should I have gone to her? I wondered. But the answer came that I should not.

She continued to sit perfectly still, her little lilac dress dancing gently around her knees. She became aware of it and tried in vain to hold it down with her right hand. She grew frustrated and let it go.

Then she spoke again. But she did not call out a name this time. Rather, it sounded from my hiding place as if she were conversing with someone. I pushed back the branches still further. Who could it be? At first, I thought that Michael must have returned, but I knew at once that I was wrong – Michael possessed a presence that was impossible to mistake. I always knew whenever he was near. His bearing was worthy of the greatest of warriors, and when he moved it was as if the clouds were following him. No. Michael was not with Lily. Then who?

She spoke quietly at first. I could see the back of her head where she sat on the garden bench as I had left her. Was she still reading from the book? No. It was closed by her side.

Her voice grew louder. She sounded angry now:

"Who are you anyway? Why do I never get to see you? Are you God? Or do you want me to think you are? You could be the devil for all I know, teasing me and joking with my soul. Just like you did with poor Eve. How was she to know what you were up to with your craft and sophistry? She believed what you told her. Was that such a crime? She did not think she was doing wrong. She was curious. Curious for knowledge. What was wrong with that? And now you think you will fool me, do you? That I shall do what you want, and believe it to be my own choice. Well, you have chosen the wrong woman this time. I know the difference between good and bad, I have experienced them both already. I am a woman of the twenty-first century, not a wet behind the ears child of nature. I have seen your type in the dock before. Bad through and through, always trying to make trouble, pervert justice, expose goodness and truth as a lie. I shan't let you do it this time, do you hear me? I shan't!"

Did this woman really understand me so well? To listen to her shout out her feelings from the depths of her soul shocked me like a bolt of lightning. It should have been me sitting there expressing the thoughts which had been locked inside my subconscious for too long. But instead it took a young woman, how was it she put it, a woman of the twenty-first century to say what I should have been saying. Did I not deserve a defence? Was I toying with my own mitigation when I questioned God's motives and my capacity for choice? Surely that was not enough? Yet perhaps that was all I was capable of, as a "wet behind the ears child of nature"? Perhaps the intellect had moved on since my time on Earth?

And yet, I fear she may be mistaken. I should have known the difference between good and bad. After all, I had lived with pure goodness all my life until then. And not just a diluted form of it such as this woman must have known. Not words of affection spoken when everything seemed to be going well. Not deeds of apparent moral fibre, performed as a means to a personally beneficial end. Not experiences of pleasure at the sight of well manicured gardens and admirably constructed buildings. Not gestures of sacrifice, made for the sake of a carefully chosen cause.

My life knew nothing of personal gain or selfish desire – until I sinned. I should not have needed to experience badness in order to recognise it. It was there all the time, by virtue of its absence, by contrast. Adam knew that. I did not. I chose to eat fruit from the forbidden tree, and if I were coerced, I sinned in choosing to listen.

God forbid that he is trying to coerce the girl now, too! Could it be that he has come into my garden once again, disguised as a serpent? She seemed to think that she was addressing the devil. Is that not what she said?

I threw aside the branches of my hiding place and ran towards the garden bench where she had been seated. But she was no longer there. There remained only a crumpled copy of a book that suddenly did not matter to me. I had to find her. It was my duty to protect her from the evil, which had already wrecked my life.

Frantically, I searched the ground for a sign of the venomous enemy. But there was nothing to see. He must have left when she did, slithering through the soil, which God had provided for his camouflage.

As I stood staring at the ground beneath my feet, suddenly it began to change: cracks emerged, small at first, but growing into large open crevices. And the sky, which until then had been clear blue, became black. I fought to make out surroundings that I knew so well, but all I could see was my own silhouette. I took a step forward, fearful that my foot would slip into one of the openings and I would be swallowed up. As I moved, the earth trembled under me. I ran on in the direction of the archway, her only possible means of retreat, but what to do when I reached it? I had never left this garden since I came here. And although I had convinced myself that it was my place of exile, my punishment, I knew suddenly that I had actually made it my refuge. The truth was, I was afraid to leave.

I thought of calling out to her, urging her back to the safety of the only place I knew. We could overcome the enemy together. Hadn't she said that she would not let him make trouble this time? Goodness, how she had shouted it out! Like a wild animal! With no fear in her voice at all! Just strength and bravery. If only I had been more like her. Oh God, why didn't you make Eve more like Lily? You could have saved your Paradise then.

She would know where to run to. She would have a plan. She was used to his type, had seen them before, bad through and through. She did not need me. Why should she?

I would stay. She would have a better chance without me, just like Adam would have had. How could I have been so foolish as to think I could be of assistance to a strong woman like her?

I turned around slowly to retreat into my garden, when suddenly the darkness disappeared as quickly as it had come, to be replaced by a sky as clear and sparkling blue as Lily's eyes. And where the ground had been cracking open moments before, now there was firm but moist soil the like of which I had not seen since I left Eden.

But there was something about the place I did not recognise. The trees seemed greener and more voluminous, the flowers were scattered here and there as if their seeds had been showered from the mountains that overhung them.

Mountains. I had not seen mountains here before. It was then I realised that I had wandered beyond the archway which had served to separate me from the beyond for so long, since – what had she said, she was a woman of the twenty-first century? It was longer than I thought. I had left my garden. I was in unknown territory.

But, strangely, I was not afraid. It was as if I had left Adam's side once again, and wandered off to an area which I knew was unfamiliar to me, forbidden, even if only by me this time, yet I was confident in myself. I knew that, should I be tempted to do wrong, I would not be persuaded. However much I was coerced, I would stand strong. I would not shout like the girl, but I would quietly say "No!" and walk away.

I strode out purposefully without any idea where I was heading. That did not matter, though. For the moment, it was enough that I was going somewhere. The sun was shining and for once I could feel it warming me. And as I focused on a large, pine-clad mountain straight ahead of me, my spirits were strangely lifted with an expectation I thought I had lost many, many years before.

Could it be my imagination, or was there a building in the distance, high and imposing, unlike the small hut that had been our home, Adam's and mine, after we left Eden? I rubbed my eyes with the backs of my hands and looked again. Yes, there was certainly something there. It was like nothing I had ever seen before. But then, my experiences of anything other than open spaces were limited.

We had lived a simple life of exile with our children, seldom venturing away from our immediate environment. Adam had spent most of his time ploughing the fields while I looked after our children. Their births had been difficult and had left me frail, so I could not help my husband the way I used to, back in Eden, back in the beginning. But he never complained. That was not his way. He was silent sometimes, and I knew then that he was remembering our former happiness. I did the same, frequently.

Our home, if I can call it that, was built by Adam. He used materials from the fields, such as straw and cow dung, and wood from the forest. When it rained, it let in water in places, and in the summer it smelled damp. We were novices in most aspects of survival, once we had been stripped of the protection which had been our gift from God. As the years went by and we accustomed ourselves to the humdrum life of mere mortals, we expanded our horizons, and gradually a small community developed. Most of the homes were built like ours, rough and unsophisticated, but we took pride in them nevertheless.

But what I saw before me now was as different from those dwellings as it is possible to imagine. In all my years on Earth, there was only one building I saw which in any way compared to this one. It was a church, built high up on the brow of a hill beside our home, which was erected in memory of my son, Abel. Abel had been a God-fearing boy and man, and it seemed fitting to provide him in death with a place of rest which did justice to his belief and his nature. It took many hands and many years to erect it, and even then it was somewhat lacking in refinement. But, to us, it was the most beautiful and glorious building we had ever seen.

The thought of the church made my eyes cloud over and obliterated the building in the distance. When I had blinked away the tears, I turned my gaze skywards, fearful of another reminder of something I had chosen to forget. There I saw a rainbow, arched high over the rooftop, with colours that melted into each other like the reflection of wild flowers in a sunlit lake. At that moment, it seemed as if a host of angels had left it there as a signpost for me to follow. And I did.

25

The closer I came to the building, the more hopeful I grew that I would find Lily again. She had come this way, I was certain.

It had the texture of rock made from sand, and it looked as if it might crumble if I were to touch it. There was a door in the centre, which was made from an old oak tree, just as ours had been, only much, much larger and smoother. As I approached it, I noticed that it was ajar.

Should I enter? Was it safe? All of a sudden I was reminded of the tree from which I had plucked the forbidden fruit. Hadn't its bark been similar in colour and texture to this door? And what sins had it housed behind an innocent veneer?

I hesitated. Recognising temptation was not as easy as I had anticipated. Once inside the building, it might be too late. After all, he was unlikely to return again as a serpent, wasn't he? He was too cunning for that. I would see through his disguise, and back away. No, he could be anything this time, and any-where.

And yet, God had not forbidden me to enter; in fact He had said nothing to me at all. Sometimes it felt as if He had deserted me completely. Besides, I would be acting out of good motives, wouldn't I? Not from some curious, defiant desire, like before.

I pushed the door open and walked in confidently. The room was so large that our entire home would have fitted inside it, with space to spare. Everywhere I looked, I found symmetry: in the stone slabs which covered the ground, in the four white walls which ended at a ceiling held up with long, thick beams of wood, in the pairs of glass windows, pinned open to display line after line of pine trees growing on the mountains.

"Eve!"

The sound of a voice startled me. I looked swiftly around the room, but I could see no-one.

"Eve!"

I was sure of it this time.

"Who's there?" I asked nervously, half expecting to see a snake slithering across the floor towards me.

"We have been waiting for you. What took you so long?"

I scanned the room for a sign, any sign, but there was nothing. It was empty of furniture, but for a large wooden table in the corner of the room.

Yet there was something familiar about the voice, like the sound of wind whistling through the trees late at night when all else is still and the world is sleeping.

"Where are you?" I asked.

"We are all upstairs," came the reply.

I opened a door to my left, and followed a long, narrow corridor until I reached a staircase in the centre of another room. It was a large, imposing staircase, which must have taken many men to build. But, perhaps that was not necessary in Purgatory. It could even be my own imagination that had created it. How was I to know? Adam was not there to explain it to me. I only knew what Michael told me, and that was very little. Michael did not use many words. He communicated in other ways. Perhaps it was my fault – I had not wanted to know. No. I had been afraid to understand.

It had happened like this. I grew old, so old that I forgot how many years had passed. I had lived to see my own children die before me. There is such hardship in that. It cannot be meant to happen. It is unnatural. I said so to Adam, but he did not agree with me. Age was unimportant, he told me.

"What matters," he said "is the maturity of one's soul. Therein lies the grief, the hardship; to witness one's child's inability to develop spiritually."

I knew that he was thinking of Cain when he spoke to me thus. It pierced him like a sword to discover that his own son had murdered another of his sons – his favourite son. And, worse than Cain's capacity for murder was his motive – fraternal jealousy. He could not bear the goodness he saw in Abel. Our dear, sweet Abel. When our child was taken from us, I convinced myself that God was punishing Adam and me for our sins – my sin. Adam had no answer, but I knew that he wondered too.

Then, one morning, I awoke earlier than usual. It must have been about four o'clock. Adam was lying beside me. Our dog, Jess, had made himself a comfortable hole in the straw mattress upon which we slept, and was nuzzling his head into Adam's chest. I patted his smooth black coat and turned towards my husband. He looked too peaceful to wake, so instead I put out my hand to caress his forehead.

It was the coldness of his skin that disturbed me first. I had felt deathly flesh before: smooth in texture, but limp and empty, like paralysis. Life had stopped flowing through his veins. My

Adam was gone from me. I lifted his left arm, now heavy with death, and placed it around my shoulders, just as he would have done, knowing that it would be the last time I would feel my husband's arm around me.

It did not take long for me to die after that. Too long, I often thought. But God was kind to me. He let me live out my final days peacefully and without pain. I deserved nothing more. I had caused the death of my husband, my children, and the rest of mankind. God had told us what the consequences of my action would be. I had led us all to death and soon it would be my turn too.

But what then? Was I to be reunited with my loved ones? Were we all to live together again, joyful as we had been in the beginning, Adam and I, only this time in the knowledge that our happiness would last for all eternity?

I had no Adam to take my questions to anymore. There was no-one left to console me in my state of desolation. Day by day I grew firmer in my resolution that I was not worthy of the after-life of which Adam had spoken so often. Michael had explained it to him when we left Eden. He talked to Adam constantly back then. Sometimes I listened, but mostly I did not care to hear. Perhaps even then the seed of my conviction was beginning to grow. But once Adam had gone, it came to fruition.

I did not deserve my husband's everlasting love. I did not deserve happiness. I did not deserve another chance. I did not deserve to see my children again. I deserved nothing. And a state of nothingness is what I chose.

I died alone. How do I know? Because I saw myself drifting away as clearly as if I had been my own twin, watching furtively from the end of the bed. Jess was lying close to me, as he always did, licking my face with his cool, pink tongue, whimpering quietly and nudging my arm with his wet nose. But I did not respond. I continued to lie motionless until hours turned into days. Had it not been for Jess's loud bark, I would probably have decomposed into the straw mattress like a dead bird in its nest.

Instead, I was given a decent burial in the church on the hill where my Abel lay. I continued to watch it all from my invisible viewpoint, never asking myself what would become of what was left of me, until he came back – Michael, God's archangel, the advocate for human souls.

He swept me up in his arms and we flew through the sky, upwards, upwards, light as a breeze.

"Eve!" He whispered to me. "It is your time now. Are you ready to go?"

That brought me back to myself. I was still Eve. I continued to exist in some form or other. I had not been granted the nothingness for which I had pleaded. I had a choice.

26

I likened the mighty staircase to a ladder, set up on earth, and winding upwards until it reached at the top to heaven. I hesitated at the foot as if it held the secret of Creation. But was it a secret I wished to discover?

The voice had called to me from above. They were all there, it had said. If I wanted to find out who was calling my name, I would have to climb the staircase.

I treaded cautiously at first, but the higher I ascended, the more my confidence grew. With every step, I was being transformed into an elegant, sophisticated woman like Lily. I felt as if I were dressed in a flowing silk gown, cut off at the shoulder, instead of a dull-white, shapeless tunic dress which I had put together myself. Of course, my clothes had always been simple by necessity. That was how it was back then. We made the best use of materials that were available to us and served to preserve the modesty which had been inflicted upon us by my actions.

When I was deposited by Michael in Purgatory, it surprised me at first to discover that I seemed to have a body, a clothed body, much as I had appeared when I was young. Not the feeble old woman who had given up on life many years before. It occurred to me that I must have chosen to appear this way and that my appearance was no more than that. How else was it possible for the physical to survive but in the imagination? But what was it that was doing the imagining if not a physical entity, a brain? And surely that would have ceased to exist with the rest of my body?

I expect the girl knew the answer to that. No doubt knowledge had advanced considerably since my day. What matter? I was here and whatever I believed to exist, including myself, existed in some form for so long as I believed it to be so.

And at that moment, I imagined myself to be gliding gracefully up a staircase and aglow with an expectation that I would be greeted at the top by a fanfare of trumpets and a host of God's worthiest angels.

I was mistaken. The landing was empty but for a long narrow wooden bench underneath a painting of a woman wearing a crown and surrounded by red shapes like diamonds. On the bench there was a bowl of fruit of every description – some I had never seen before. But I would not be tempted this time. Next to the bowl of fruit was a half-empty jug of water and a glass.

Four doors led off from the landing, two on either side of me. There were numbers on all the doors: 11, 12, 13 and 14.

Door 12 was closest to me, on my left, but for some reason I did not wish to enter that room. Instead, I headed towards door 11. The symmetry of the number appealed to me, the way it read the same backwards as forwards.

"You knew where to find us." The voice was quieter now, almost a whisper. I pushed open the door and walked into room 11.

I was not prepared for what I saw. It was as if I were staring at a starry sky late at night through an opening framed with curved beams of golden light shaped like rainbows, with a gentle breeze carrying towards me the scent of smouldering pine logs infused with herbs.

At first I found it hard to make sense of what I was seeing, but gradually shapes began to emerge out of the darkness. I had seen candles in church before, but never had I witnessed so many all at once. There must have been a hundred or more of varying shapes and sizes glowing around the room. Their flames burnt still until I moved and then they danced in a frenzy of activity until I was motionless again. There were no windows in the room to offer light, there was only the candlelight, but I could see enough to know that I was not alone.

It was easy to pick out Michael – I knew him so well, and his presence was unmistakable. The other two I thought I had not seen before. Their faces were rounded, their skin was pale and their eyes were powder blue. But they did not look alike. The one closest to me had long fair hair which he kept pushing behind his ears. He was dressed in a coral-coloured coat which reached to the ground and he seemed to be laughing at something. His companion, who was standing next to Michael, had dark, curly hair, which made him look at first glance like a woman.

"You do not remember us," he said. His voice was calm and gentle and he spoke as if he were uttering a prayer. The sound of it took me back much further than had his appearance.

"You came to us in Paradise. I do remember you," I said, proud of my memory, "You are Gabriel."

He seemed pleased with me, and smiled saying simply:
"Eve!"

As he spoke my name, I noticed that his cheeks reddened into a blush.

"And what about me?" laughed his companion, "Can you tell me who I am too?"

He looked hard into my eyes as he addressed me as Michael was in the habit of doing, and then, before I had time to answer him, he said:

"Yes, that's right. I am Raphael," and he laughed again.

In truth, I did not remember him, and I wondered whether in fact he knew that, too. But, for whatever reason, he chose it to be this way, and I was happy to reply:

"I am pleased to see you again, Raphael."

All the while, Michael looked on from his standpoint by the wall, mighty but tender like a loving parent watching over his young. Somehow I had not expected to find him here, contained within the confines of a building. He should be outside with the wind and the mountains and the trees. Could this be where he came whenever he disappeared?

This time, he did not answer my thought, but instead he said:

"You came here to look for Lily didn't you, Eve?"

I felt ashamed that for a moment I had forgotten the reason I was there. Had I sinned again? I wondered.

"Forgive us. We took you by surprise. It is our fault, not yours."

It was Raphael who spoke this time.

"She is always too harsh on herself," added Michael, as if he meant to chastise me. I was used to that.

"Have you seen her, Michael? Is she here?" I asked.

Michael's face grew solemn, as if he had bad news to tell me. I knew him too well to be mistaken. My mind raced through numerous possibilities: she had been tricked by the serpent into some wrongdoing; she had been deserted by her husband and now she wanted nothing but standstill; she felt I had let her down when I did not respond to her call; she refused to see me again; she had been chastised by God for a sin she had committed on Earth of which I was unaware and he had sent her to that other place; she had never existed at all.

"What is it, Michael?" I pleaded into the heavy silence. "Tell me – please!" I was truly humble now. Gone was my stoic determination, my indignant certainty that only I knew what was right for me.

"Are you ready?" asked Raphael of me, brushing his hand gently across my cheek.

"She is ready." Michael answered for me.

27

They led me between the candles as if we were caught up in a heavenly maze. The room was larger than I had realised, and where I had imagined there would be a wall separating us from the room next door, room 12, I found that there was only a screen of white vapour to act as a dividing line.

I felt as if I were being led through the clouds, just as it had seemed when Michael had first brought me from Earth to this place, this state of existence.

In an instant, the air had cleared again, and I could see all around me. It was bright, this other room, and instead of candles, brilliant sunshine lit the room through two large, open windows. My eyes were drawn at once to the view out of the window to my right. A tall, sombre mountain monopolised the scenery like a heavy shadow of its neighbours. Only this mountain seemed barren, devoid of habitation of any description. It stood in stark contrast to the lightness of the room and caused my spirits to drop as suddenly as they had risen.

It was then I noticed the bed. A large, white bed with four twisted oak poles, one in each corner. I had no reason to avoid it. It meant nothing to me. So I peered with curiosity inside the white cotton sheets.

Her skin seemed paler than I remembered against the

whiteness of the pillow. And her long, flaxen hair rested around her face like a crop of corn on a summer's day. I wanted to call out to her, but I knew she would not hear me. Her eyes were closed and the energy had gone from her demeanour. I thought of Adam, lying motionless on our straw bed, the same bed which had housed my own frail body too, when death had finally come.

But, death? How could this be death, when death had already taken her? Had I not seen her, spoken to her? Had Michael not explained to her this mid-way stage?

Michael leaned over her, stroking her hair. He looked so troubled that I dared not disturb him with my questions.

"Oh, Lily!"

Was I mistaken or was that a woman's voice I had heard speaking to the girl? I looked across the bed to where a figure was seated in a large white armchair. It surprised me that I had not noticed her before. She was holding Lily's hand in hers as she spoke to her. She was crying.

"Lily, why?"

The girl did not reply. In despair, the woman let the girl's hand fall, pushed back her chair and ran to the open window beside me.

Instinctively I placed a comforting arm around her shoulder:

"I am sure she can hear you," I whispered into her ear.

The woman made no reply, but continued to stare out of the window towards the mountains, lost in her thoughts.

"Keep trying," I encouraged her, but still she remained silent.

"Mrs. Scott, you need to get some rest. You have been in this room for hours now."

The man who spoke succeeded where I had failed; the woman turned around to face him, saying:

176

"I came as quickly as I could when I received the call. But somehow I knew already that it would be too late."

Her words were interrupted by quiet but uncontrolled sobs which she tried to conceal with the back of her hand.

"He should have told me before," she wept, "as soon as he regained consciousness. She needed me, and I was not here for her."

Her sobbing grew louder as if she no longer cared what effect it would have on anyone else. The only person she would wish to protect from her despair could not hear it anyway. So what matter? I knew her thoughts as if they were my own, for once they had been.

"Doctor Vio, are you a religious man?" the mother asked when eventually her tears had subsided.

The elderly man did not respond immediately. He seemed uncertain of an answer. I watched as he rubbed his eyes, then ran a hand over the top of his bald head.

"Doctor Vio," urged the woman, "I would like to know."

"I would like to know too, Doctor Vio." I called out, angered suddenly by the manner in which I was being ignored by everyone, even Michael.

The doctor looked up from the floor to where the woman stood beside me. He was concerned for the woman, that much was clear. But there was something about the expression in his eyes that reminded me of my husband just before he told me that we were to leave Paradise.

"Mrs Scott, there is something I…"

The woman did not allow him time to finish his words, but interrupted them before they reached her with:

"You do not need to tell me. I know already. I saw the change come over her face a while ago. It was as if a violent thunder-storm had passed, and the air was suddenly still and warm again. Do you understand what that feels like, Doctor Vio?"

"I understand it!" I shouted out impulsively. "And Lily would, too."

"I heard God speak to me at that moment," the woman continued. "Or if it were not Him, then perhaps it was an angel. Lily believed in angels, you know. It was like a whisper, but without words, as if a gentle breeze was carrying a message to me from the other side of the bed."

The doctor approached the large white bed, which housed his patient, and lifted Lily's arm by the wrist. He held it still for a time before returning it to her side.

All the while, Michael had not stirred from his watchful position on the other side of the bed. It was as if he were in a trance, oblivious to everything but the girl. I wanted to call out to him, but I knew he would not answer me. I was too unimportant for the contents of this room. Each had their own role to play, no doubt, in His great scheme of things. Was it surprising that He had chosen to leave me out? Of course not. I was not worthy of this gathering. I was an impostor. It was right that they should all ignore me. The girl deserved their attention more than I, after all. Something had happened to her since she left me in the garden. I was right to have been concerned for her. If I had learned anything in Paradise, it was how to predict danger. Perhaps I had recognised it even back then, but I chose to ignore the warning that sounded in my head. I would not commit that sin again.

"Lily!" I shouted out in the direction of the bed, "It is I, Eve! What has become of you? What are you doing here in this place?"

I watched for a sign of movement, of recognition, but there was none. The girl did not reply. It was no surprise. I had not expected an answer, I spoke because I had to do something and that was all I could think of. A state of impasse was no longer an alternative for me, even if it had become so for the girl. I stared down at her motionless frame swathed in white cottons, her eyes tightly closed as if she were sleeping, her limp arms on either side of her, like weights anchoring an empty shell to a sea bed. What did it mean? Death within death? Was it possible?

I looked helplessly towards Michael but still he ignored me. Perhaps the doctor could explain; he must have witnessed death often and if that was his role on Earth then why should it cease here in Purgatory?

I looked at his anxious, confused face and wondered what conflict was keeping him suspended here, as we all were. It was obvious why the woman had come, she would not leave her daughter. That I understood. They looked so alike, she and the girl, there was no questioning their relationship. How often I had wished that I could follow Abel when he departed, but it was not to be. Perhaps I was not as strong as this woman, perhaps I was stronger. I did not have the answer. I had no answers at all any more, just questions, and the only person who seemed able to help me with those, after years and years and years of stagnation was now stagnant herself in a sterile bed.

"Go to her!" I whispered suddenly into the mother's ear and for the first time she responded to me. She sat down quietly on the end of the bed, holding her daughter's covered toes in both her hands and stroking the soles of her feet. I watched the scene as if I were abstracted from it – the small white shape in the centre of what had now become a circle of intense affection all around her, the doctor on one side of her, Michael on the other and the mother at the base. Above the bed, a wooden crucifix was pinned to the wall by a single nail. Strange that I had not noticed it before. I sensed a power in the gathering beyond my previous experiences and I wanted to be part of it. So I started to move towards them when I noticed a wooden door to my left. It was ajar, so that I could see both sides of it at the same time. The number 12 was visible at its centre and beyond it I could see the landing through which I had passed on my way to room 11. There was the seat against the wall, and the brightly-coloured painting above it, but the fruit in the bowl and the half empty jug of water had been removed. Was there someone else here?

I walked determinedly through the open doorway and onto the landing. Ahead of me was a closed door numbered 13, to its left another door numbered 14 and to my left was door 11 through which I had passed earlier. I had my bearings again. The staircase should be on my right. I turned my head in what I believed to be the direction of the staircase. It was an impulsive response, or so I thought. Perhaps I sensed that someone was there, climbing the stairs, perhaps I heard a movement, perhaps the atmosphere had been altered slightly by friction, perhaps He had whispered to me that it would be so. Yet I swear on the souls of my Adam and Abel that I had not expected it to be her – Lily, the girl.

28

She walked towards me as if her energy and vivacity had never disappeared. Her lilac dress swung around her body as she walked, and she pushed her long flaxen hair behind her ears to reveal a glowing bronzed face once again.

"Eve!" she called out as soon as she saw me. "What are you doing here?"

"I came to look for you," I replied, uncertain what to say next.

"And you found me," she laughed, unmistakably happy to see me again.

"But what happened to you?" I asked with caution.

"I wanted to find Harry – my husband – and this was the last place I saw him. That was the room they gave us." She pointed towards door 12. "I thought it was an hotel then. We were supposed to be on holiday."

She spoke as if she were trying to remember a fragmented dream.

"But I was wrong, Eve, wasn't I?"

She did not wait for a reply, but went on :

"That means that he must be here too, doesn't it?"

I knew that she wanted me to answer her this time, because she looked hard into my eyes after she had finished speaking.

"Perhaps," I replied half-heartedly. She recognised my uncertainty and clung on to it as if she were in danger of disappearing if it were not resolved.

"Perhaps?" She spoke the word more loudly than I had. "You mean he may not be here, in this place? Or do you mean he may not be here at all?"

In truth I had no answers to her questions. Indeed, I had not heard mention of Harry until then. I knew she had a husband, Michael had told me that, but it had not occurred to me to wonder about him.

"I have no idea where your husband is," I answered her, "but I shall help you to look for him if you wish."

She seemed pleased with my reply and began to walk towards door 12.

"This is the first place to look," she said with renewed confidence.

I was unused to being in situations where I was obliged to think as quickly as this. I had always left it to Adam to assess problems for us. That is not to say that I did not reflect on them. Often. But then in my own time, with little to distract me and with nothing more to lose. Or so I believed. Yet somehow I forced myself to analyse the events which were following one another too hastily for me, and I resolved that the girl must not enter room 12 under any circumstances.

"There is no point in looking in that room," I said as calmly and with as much authority as possible, "I have just come from it and your husband is certainly not there."

She accepted what I said with such trust in me that I wondered for a moment whether I was doing right. I had to go back into the room alone and try to understand for myself before I was able to help her. So I said:

"Why don't you look outside and I shall search the building?"

She nodded her agreement and disappeared down the stairs.

I held no image of what I expected to see when I re-entered the room. Therefore, when I found that everything was as I had left it, I was not surprised, even when I saw Lily's frail form still lying motionless in the bed. How could it be otherwise? Yet how could it be so?

"Think back awhile, Eve." It was Michael, finally. He walked towards me with the speed and grace of a bird in flight and hurried me out of the room onto the landing whence I had come.

"Have you forgotten how you watched yourself in death?" he asked, although he knew my answer. I shook my head and he went on:

"Then why is it so difficult for you to understand, Eve, you of all people?"

I thought for a moment then answered:

"Because the girl is no longer a mortal who is experiencing death on Earth. She is in Purgatory, dead already, you told her so yourself. I heard you. So how can she die again?"

Michael walked towards the staircase and I feared that he might disappear before I had an answer. But I was wrong. He stopped suddenly and turned around so that we stood face to face, strength to strength, soul to soul. Who would be the first to break the silence?

"Dear Eve," he whispered at last, "how you have changed!"

"Have I?" I asked, without a shadow of the self-consciousness which had brought me down before. "But, what of Lily?" I went on.

Michael smiled and touched my cheek with the back of his hand, and I thought for some reason he seemed proud of me just then.

"You are right, Eve. I did tell Lily that she was in Purgatory, as you are. But I kept something back from her. I had to, for her sake."

This was not the kind of answer I was used to hearing from the mighty Archangel. It was confused, unclear, incoherent.

"What are you telling me, Michael?"

"I am trying to tell you, Eve, that the girl – Lily – is not dead."

29

"I would like to return to the garden," I said softly and
Michael knew not to argue with me. He had seen me
like this before, suddenly introspective, desirous of silence for
however long it took me to absorb what I had been told and
make sense of it for myself.

When we left the building and were outside again my first
thought was of Lily. What should I do if we saw her searching
for her husband? What should I say?

The alarming prospect urged me on at a faster pace and
in moments we were back within the security of my private
garden, sitting side by side, Michael and I, as if we had never
left. Thoughts of Lily dropped away from my mind like melting
clouds and before long it was as if she had never existed.
Perhaps she had not. What matter? I no longer cared to know.
There was a great deal of the world I did not understand. It was
not my role to be a thinker.

"You are wrong, Eve." They were Michael's first words since
we had left the building. "You have a great capacity for contemplation."

I shrugged my shoulders and stared down at my feet. Did
Michael still not realise that I was just a simple unsophisticated
woman? I had not been educated like the girl, I did not have

the ability to analyse complex arguments and reach subtle conclusions. My life had been very different from hers. Little things had pleased me – nurturing plants and delighting in their growth, watching a bird fly through the sky, tilling the soil with my bare hands, wiping my Adam's sweating brow.

"Then what is keeping you here?" asked Michael with a smile. I realised at once what he meant. How could he have shared with me my half-existence here in Purgatory without knowing, as I did, the answer to that question.

"You are referring to my thoughts, I see that. But where do they take me? I exist in a timeless vacuum of uncertainty, spiralling through spacelessness in ever increasing circles of thought, leading me nowhere but ever deeper, driving me within myself until I can no longer see the beauty all around me, as I once did. Is that my capacity for contemplation of which you talk, Michael?"

Michael looked downcast, as if he knew he was getting nowhere with me.

"You cannot find your answers on your own, Eve!" he cried in frustration as if it were a final plea.

"Then why can you not explain things to me yourself? You and your Master have all the answers, don't you?" I sounded like the girl now, angry and strong but confused all the same.

He took my hand and pressed it to his lips. The gesture brought me back to myself and I remembered who I was and who Michael was too. I had hurt him with my critical words. I had forgotten his godly role. His aim was to save souls in death, to advocate before God on their behalf. Had I not seen him cry tears over souls he had lost? Had I not watched him battle for my own?

"Forgive me, Michael," I whispered.

"That is the first time you have spoken those words to me," he replied without a suggestion of criticism. I was suddenly ashamed, as if it was Adam sitting beside me, personifying the wrong I had done. Only this time, I had put it right.

"I can try to explain things, Eve, but I cannot make you understand. Just as I can read your thoughts but I cannot create them. That is up to you."

He paused for a moment to make sure that I was listening correctly, then he went on:

"You make it hard for me to help you sometimes, you know. Think of the times I have begun to speak of Adam to you and you have chastised me for it, as if you could not bear the mention of his name."

He spoke the truth although I could not explain why I reacted as I did, either to Michael or to myself, so I said nothing but allowed him to continue.

"And now it is the same with the girl, Lily. You have decided that you do not want to hear any more of her. So tell me, Eve, how can I explain when you will not listen?"

I put my hands to my ears as I was in the habit of doing at times like this and Michael did what he normally did, he got up to leave. The difference was that this time I would not let him go.

"Wait!" I shouted, clutching at his long white sleeve. "You said that she is not dead – Lily. How can that be?"

Michael looked at me as if he had given sight to a blind man or stumbled upon water in the desert. He sat down beside me again, and I waited. He closed his eyes and I sensed he was asking Him for clarity.

"We took you into room 12, Gabriel, Raphael and I, because we thought you were ready."

"Ready for what?"

"To transcend the barriers which keep you here, separated from your former existence."

"You mean I went back to Earth?"

"In a sense, yes, although you were still here at the same time. Similarly, Lily transcended those barriers in order to come here from Earth. Do you understand?"

"But you say that she is not dead. Then how can she be in both existences at the same time?"

He closed his eyes again and it seemed as if his outline was becoming hazy and evaporating into the air. He opened his eyes again.

"Lily is not dead, but she is close to death. What you saw was a room where Lily is a patient. The doctor is trying to save her life and her mother, Mary, is praying for her salvation."

"Then her mother is keeping her alive?"

"Mary wants what is best for her daughter, whether that be life or death. The choice is not hers, it is Lily's."

"But Lily thinks she is dead already."

"She had to understand what had happened to her. She was confused. She believed that she was as she was before the accident. It happens like that sometimes."

"But why did you not tell her that she had a choice?"

"Because she has to understand before she can decide with clarity."

"Understand what?"

"What you have to tell her, Eve."

30

It was easy for me to find her. I followed in the direction that I would have taken myself. She was sitting cross-legged under a large oak tree on the corner of the terrace, looking out towards the mountains in the distance.

"Lily!" I called, but she did not answer me. I drew nearer. "Lily!"

"I was dreaming," she said, as she opened her eyes and focused them on me. "I dreamt that I was floating on a large white fluffy cloud. It felt wonderful, peaceful but for some reason I wanted to get away. I tried to stand but my legs and arms would not move, so I relaxed back into the cloud again. Isn't it strange, Eve, that I should still dream in this place? Do you dream too?"

All I could think of was my conversation with Michael earlier, but I had no idea what it was that I should be trying to make her understand. Nevertheless I had to say something, so I replied:

"It is hard to know sometimes what is a dream and what is a reality."

"So do you think we could be dreaming this very conversation?" she asked, curious to explore the line of thought I had begun.

"It is possible," I said cautiously. "What do you think?"

"I think that my dream was just as clear as this moment, and yet there is something about the present which makes me certain that I am not dreaming it. What can it be, Eve?"

"Perhaps it is the contemplation which gives you certainty. It is important that we think. It keeps us alive. I did not realise that myself until a moment ago when I was speaking with Michael."

"Michael? Has he returned?" She stood up and looked excitedly around her. "Where is he?"

"He wanted me to find you."

"And you did. I wish I could find Harry as easily."

Her husband. Michael had not referred to him. I had assumed that he was here somewhere. And yet, it may be that he was still alive. Lily believed that he had been here, in the building with her. But how could she be certain?

"Lily, are you sure that he was here with you?"

"Of course I am!" she answered confidently. "This is the very terrace where we danced in the moonlight. This is the very tree Harry hid behind. This is the building that I thought was our hotel. That is the archway which took us to Reception and our room. Room 12 overlooking this terrace. The room you looked in earlier. There was a large white bed in the centre and two French windows looking out towards the mountains and the church."

"The church?" I repeated, and I could see that Lily was formulating the same thought as I.

I took her hand as if we were two children lost on a sandy beach, and together we stared into the distance hoping for a sign of something that we had missed.

190

And there it was, glorious to behold, rising from the ground like a mighty warrior battling for our souls, beckoning us to draw closer and see for ourselves the beauty which its majestic walls embraced.

How was it possible that we had overlooked it for so long when it was there all the time, towering over us?

I did not need Lily's confirmation to know that we were of one mind – we had to visit the church. What did we expect to find there? I cannot say, but we headed towards it as if it held the secret of all eternity.

We clung to each other as we set off from the terrace. It was new territory for me, but Lily approached it with the mastery of someone who had been that way before.

"This is the best way," she said as she guided me past an area of arid, dark land towards a grassy path I had not spotted.

"Keep hold of my hand." And she climbed a steep hill like a young deer being stalked by hunters. Higher and higher we rose, occasionally losing sight of our goal, but not for long.

"Can we stop awhile?" I asked, dizzy with the heights we were achieving.

"Not until we reach the top," she called to me over her left shoulder. The top was closer than I had anticipated. It came upon us suddenly, around a final bend and we were there.

The church was larger than I had imagined it would be. As I stood outside its walls I thought it must be the most glorious spectacle in all Creation. But my experiences were limited: the only House of God I had known was built of rough materials by men who knew nothing of architecture or finery of any kind. This building gave the impression of years of planning and drawing and crafting to the very last detail. I had never seen its like, and at that moment I felt honoured to stand before it as a witness to its greatness.

Without thinking, I fell to my knees and placed my hands together. I have no idea how long I knelt there before I was disturbed by Lily's hand upon my shoulder.

"Eve!" she whispered softly as if she were afraid to break my train of thought, "Are you ready to go inside?"

"Of course," I replied, taking the hand she offered me.

Fortunately, the door was ajar. Otherwise I believe we would have found it too heavy to open ourselves. Once inside, it closed behind us and suddenly we were immersed in utter darkness.

Neither of us moved. Silently we stood hand in hand, hoping that it would not take long for us to acclimatise to the absence of bright daylight that had been shut out.

Gradually shapes began to emerge – a circular window first of all, high up to our right. Then a cross below it, as tall as a young apple tree. There were three small steps leading to an altar and in the corner stood a pulpit intricately carved out of smooth dark wood.

We walked towards the altar as if we had lost possession of our free will. Had we been attacked on our way by a flock of vultures eager for our blood still we would not have been deterred. And yet, when we reached the altar, both of us stopped abruptly and lowered our heads like repentant sinners. Perhaps we were. Certainly I was. Who knows what wrongs the girl had committed in her time?

When I raised my head I could see more clearly. There was a huge white candle beside the cross, which gave off a golden glow of light and illuminated a table in front of it. On the table were three place settings consisting of large pewter plates and goblets, and wooden-handled knives. The plates were empty, but the goblets were filled to the brim with what looked like red wine. At the head of the table stood a heavy high-backed wooden chair, beautifully carved like the pulpit. Three small plain wooden chairs were positioned next to each other along one length of the table but its opposite side was empty.

I turned to Lily for guidance, assuming that this was not the spectacle for her that it was for me. But all she did was to stare ahead of her in bewilderment. I had hoped that she would call out, perhaps as she had done in the garden when she thought she was alone. But she did not. Her face was as motionless as it had appeared in the large white bed, except that her eyes were open this time.

"Lily!" I whispered, "What should we do?"

She made no reply, so I asked myself the same question. It was not as difficult as I had thought to answer it. Without hesitation, I mounted the three steps and lowered myself as gracefully as possible into the large carved wooden chair at the head of the table.

I found that the arms of the chair were a perfect length for my own, and the upright posture which I was obliged to take on encouraged my composure in the dignified position.

Before long, I was beckoning to the girl to join me. She obeyed as if I were a goddess and she my humble servant. She sat in the chair that was furthest from me and crossed her hands on her lap. She seemed younger than she had before, innocent like a child. I wanted to run to the empty chair beside her so that she would not be alone, but somehow it did not seem the right thing to do, just as it seemed that the correct thing to do was to turn towards the empty pulpit and wait. But wait for what?

"For the trial to begin, Eve." The voice was unmistakable.

"Michael," I cried. "Where are you?"

"I am behind you," came his reply, "where you cannot see me."

To my surprise, Lily gave no sign of recognition, but continued to sit, absorbed by her solitude.

Then the rest of the church began to come into focus, as if a cloudy white vapour was disappearing. There must have been fifty pews in front of me, maybe more. Line after line of them facing towards the altar in organised reverence. I stared into the darkness trying to see them more clearly. There was no candle-light in their direction, so it was difficult to make them out at first. That was why it came as such a shock to me. I had expected the pews to be empty, but instead they were crammed with people; men, women and children of varying ages and sizes.

They did not make a sound, but sat, all of them, as if they were in attendance upon an event of the utmost importance.

How was I to know what to say? Should I address them? I had never seen so many people under one roof before. Surely this was the girl's domain. She would be in her element in a situation such as this, with an audience to await her every word with a respectful solemnity in keeping with her legal profession.

But what had I to do with gatherings like these? Throughout my time in Purgatory I had hidden myself from others on the whole. And, worst of all, they were all looking at me, I could see their eyes – curious, intrigued as if they had stumbled upon a new species.

194

I searched the pews for a face I recognised but there was none. Not even a suggestion of familiarity. They were strangers, every one. Some viewed me with fondness, but many looked upon me with hostility in their hearts, I could see that. There was no doubting that they knew who I was. Or at least, they thought they did. But what did they want from me now?

"They want to hear what Lily has to say about you."

A man in the front pew nodded his head as Michael spoke. He was an old man with an air of intelligence about his expression. I sensed that his opinions would be measured and fair, and would only be given after a great deal of consideration.

The mention of her name seemed to waken Lily from a kind of trance, and suddenly she was animated again.

"Michael?" she enquired. "Is that you?"

"Yes, Lily," he replied from his place of hiding.

"Do you remember what you were told, what we wanted you to do?"

The girl reflected for a moment as if whatever it was that she had been asked to do had momentarily slipped her mind.

"I remember," she said at last, "You wanted me to represent Eve's soul at a trial in which Eve was to be the Judge."

The girl's words pierced me like a knife. Had she not come to me as a friend, unconditionally, without an ulterior motive? Had she not persuaded me to trust in her? Had she not allowed me to believe that I could help her, too? And all the while there had been a plan. Not just any old plan – His plan, and I had been its subject once again.

I was trembling as I stood up and turned to the girl at the bottom of the table saying:

"Fie to you, you foolish girl! You serpent in a woman's clothes! Traitor to the truth!"

Did I mean what I said, or did my anger speak its own words? Who knows? Yet as soon as I had spoken, and I saw the look of horror and anxiety in the girl's face, I feared I had gone too far.

"Eve!" she cried through tears that flowed like waterfalls, "What have I done?"

I should have said: "Can't you see? You have unleashed a torrent of memories I would rather have kept locked within the depths of my mind forever." But I did not. Instead, I sat down again and lowered my head onto the table in a gesture of despair. I should have known she would run to my side and cradle me in her arms as if I were a child.

"Eve!" she said, "Forgive me if I have done you wrong. It was the voice I heard in the wilderness. He asked me to help you. He said that He needed me to persuade you and others that your soul is not lost, as you believe it to be. And I agreed to help. Then Michael led me to you and after that I forgot all about what I had promised to do. I did not even think of myself as an advocate any more. I just thought you were my friend and I yours."

I heard a collective sigh emanating from the direction of the pews, but I was left uncertain as to whether the girl spoke the truth or whether, rather, she was very good at her job. Could it be both? I doubted so.

I looked hard into her eyes as I had seen Michael do. But I was unsure what I was supposed to be looking for, so I said:

"Don't you think I am in a better position to know my own soul than you are?"

"Do you want my honest opinion?" she asked.

196

"There is no other I am prepared to listen to," I replied with caution in my voice.

"Then I shall tell you. I think that you have withdrawn into yourself for too long here. It is supposed to be a midway stage, not somewhere to stagnate and feel sorry for yourself."

"Let me be the judge of that!" I snapped back at her, thinking all the while, "Perhaps the girl is right."

"That is precisely what is wanted of you. Be the judge! Use your intellect, your capacity for analysis and decide on the facts as I shall put them!"

I was lost for words, but then I was just a simple child of nature, not an intellectual, practised at giving speeches and winning arguments like she.

"Won't you, Eve?"

What was I to answer? What did she hope to achieve? His favour perhaps? Or Michael's? Or mine?

I nodded my consent for her to go on, but remained silent, partly because I was embarrassed by the numbers who were listening to our argument.

"Thank you, Eve."

It was not the girl who spoke this time, but Michael.

"We are ready to begin!" he announced, and then all was quiet again.

31

It was not until I had left Paradise behind that I taught myself how to pray. Before then, I had not needed to close my eyes to speak to Him, for he had been there with me, as clear and distinct as my own Adam. Of course, His visits to us had been infrequent, but there was no doubting them. From the time we were banished, I never saw Him again.

Sometimes, late at night, after Adam had died, when I lay trying to sleep on my mattress of straw, I would think I saw Him begin to take shape in the darkness. I would wake from my state of half-sleep and try to recapture the image before it slipped completely from my mind's eye. But as soon as I concentrated my thoughts on what I was seeing, the shape would be lost to the darkness of the room. Probably, it had never existed outside my own creation. Even so, the experiences, however fleeting, encouraged me to believe in the possibility of seeing Him again.

Why had He abandoned us? Because we had let Him down. He had had great plans for us – we were to be the beginning of an entirely new race – beings who were as close to his ideal as possible, without reaching the status of angels. Something akin to saints I suppose you could say. And yet, a question always preyed upon my mind: what next? What did He have in store for us once we had attained the goals which He hoped we would achieve? Death was to be denied us, that much was certain. Otherwise, He would not have forbidden us from tasting from the Tree, the tragic curse of our existence. Then, what did that leave us as a possibility? A life of eternal happiness, tinged only by our fervent quest to grow ever closer to Him? Was that how Michael had begun? How were we to know when no-one ever told us? Nothing was explained. All was left half-undone, like a story with no end, or at least with a moral which it was for us to discover ourselves.

He could have helped us more. Is it blasphemous of me to say that? He who knows everything must surely be beyond the criticism of a peasant like me. We had our purpose, no doubt. Perhaps we failed to listen hard enough; we took our good fortune for granted. He tested us, and we failed.

But yet, if I had turned to Him in prayer and focused all my wasted energy upon the essence of His being, what different course might humankind have taken? Might I have been spared from producing a son who chose to slaughter his own brother? Might I still be living happily in Paradise with my Adam, instead of remaining here alone in this wretched state of unease? Might not that fearful creature, blood of sin, destruction of goodness, have been driven back whence he came, a failure in his own land? And might the human race have been spared the bitter-sweet taste of death?

Thoughts of such possibilities turned my mind toward a state of contemplation which seldom left me until, that is, I came to Purgatory. Gradually I discovered, in my later years on Earth, a stillness that I had not known before. And it was not just that old age had dulled my senses. Rather, my senses were awoken by the state of calm which I exuded. And, like sunshine at the end of a cloudy day, I bathed in the warmth of my new-found understanding.

That was how I knew that I was closer to Him than ever before. That was why I accepted when it was time for me to move on to another state of being. And so I acquiesced and came here, to this land of solitude and wondering only to find that in so doing my mind drifted further and further away from the heights it had taken me so long to achieve.

I expected more. Hadn't He promised me something great in the dark silence of my mind? Hadn't He whispered of wonders too beautiful to contemplate? Then where were they? And why was Adam not here to greet me?

There! I have said it! No need to keep it to myself any more! The one thought which has plagued me since the moment I came here is out in the open. I feel I have been let down by the one being who meant more to me than life itself. Yes, I can say that now that I have none. And now that I have said it, I could shout it out into the air from the depths of my soul, loud, louder than the girl in the garden:

"Adam, you have let me down! You have disappointed me to the point of despair! Your absence has pained my heart like a knife's edge! Why were you not here to meet me? What could be so important that you would forget about your wife?

And as for you, God, didn't you promise me, night after night, that I would join him? Isn't that what I heard you say through my tears? Isn't that what lifted my heart to new levels of contentment when he left me? Why did you mislead me so? Out of punishment, retribution? Am I not worthy of him any more?

Adam! Come to me! Find me here and show me how to live

again! Give me hope! Can you hear me? Did I need to voice it for you to understand? Did not everything about me cry out to you that I longed to be with you again, forever this time? Adam, my soul, I am here waiting for you! Let me not wait in vain!"

But it is a futile plea. So I keep it to myself, never allowing anyone to come too close to it, not even Michael. Otherwise, I fear I would break into a million pieces and float around the atmosphere like a swarm of mosquitoes, kept alive by other people's blood. It is not my way to ask for anything. Once upon a time I asked for answers, but now I have no questions to be answered. It matters not. I know he will not come. I do not need to hear Him tell me why. So I pray no more, and I never deceive myself that I hear Him speak to me.

Therefore, when the girl turned her head towards me in the church and said, "Let us first pray!" in her imperious way, I was struck to the core with confusion. And, when I looked at the many faces staring out of the half-darkness towards me, waiting for my response, I dared not disobey. So I bowed my head and closed my eyes, as I had once been in the habit of doing, and I waited.

32

It began like a breeze, away in the distance, caressing the treetops and bending their sway. Then it grew closer, whistling its way towards me, stirring the mountains with the strength of its presence. It was outside the church, fighting to enter. It was hurling its force against its walls. I dared not venture outside the confines of my enclosed state of darkness; if I opened my eyes for just one second, just long enough to confirm my surroundings, it might be lost to me forever.

A window shook, I heard a pane of glass shattering into a thousand pieces, and knew that it had come inside. It was beside me, all around me, outside me and within. I did not need to see it to know that it was there. All I had to do was listen.

"Eve!" the voice whispered, "Eve!"

The voice. I had heard it before. In Eden. Hard to forget. Quiet and gentle at first, like the voice of an angel, then gradually becoming louder as I listened to its carefully chosen words.

"Eve!" The voice continued to call my name as if it had never ceased to address me.

"Don't you remember me, Chosen Eve?"

"Go away!" I cried, crushing my ears with the palms of my

hands until I feared my head would shatter like the pane of glass. But I could no more block out the present than I could the past.

"You are too beautiful for tears, Eve," it continued. "Wipe them away and open your lovely eyes."

"NO!" I shouted from my darkness, and squeezed my eyes still tighter shut.

The voice was soft again, like trickling water in a mountain stream.

"Eve, my child! You have nothing to fear from me but the Truth. That was all I ever wanted you and Adam to understand. You deserved to know the Truth, and once you heard it, you and I became as One. Look at me, wise Eve!"

I felt a hand take mine and press it gently. It was Lily.

"Eve!" she whispered in my ear. "You prayed for His help, and He has come to help you. Don't block Him out!"

"You don't understand!" I replied through my tears.

"Yes I do," Lily said. "You are afraid. You do not want to be hurt anymore. But we are here for you, He and I. Open your eyes now, Eve! I cannot see Him without your help. I can only hear Him. And I want so much to see Him."

"Very well," I said at last. "But it is your choice, Lily, not mine. Remember that."

The voice was silent as I opened my eyes; it had not expected victory so soon. Lily watched me as if I were a guiding star. I turned my gaze in the direction the voice had taken. I sensed her do the same. She was eager for a vision of Him. She longed for an answer to her prayers. She thought I could lead her to Him, fool that she was! She should have listened to me, not to the voice. I had tried to warn her. And now it was too late.

203

She had let him in. I had let him in. God, where are You now, when we need You?

She had seen him, the girl. I did not need to look on him myself to know that. I saw it in her face. I recognised the shock, the fear, the horror at what she had done. I saw her skin turn crimson with shame as mine had once done. I watched her disappear inside herself where no one could reach her, not even him.

He had curled his wiry black body around the cross above the altar as if it were a tree. At the top of the cross, his tiny head darted from side to side, and when he spoke his long white tongue licked the air with frenzied delight.

"You see, Eve!" He laughed as he fixed his hungry eyes upon mine. "We are alike, you and I!"

33

I heard a woman screaming from the back of the church. Her terror acted like an avalanche down the lines of pews in front of her. Pandemonium broke out. The crowd surged towards the closed door which Lily and I had opened with hope not long before. It would not move now. It was locked.

Above the tumult, the serpent's laughter cracked like a whip, driving men, women and children into a state of frenzy. Only Lily and I remained silent, like conquered officers on a bloody battlefield surveying the dead.

Our spirits were broken at that moment. There were no further depths for us to reach. Neither of us cared what happened next. Impulsively, I stretched out my arms skywards, threw back my head and shouted:

"It is done, Lord! Do with me as You will!"

It was as if the ceiling had opened and the sun had fallen into the church from its place in the sky. The glare was so bright that I was forced to shield my eyes with my hand. Lily did the same. It was the first movement she had made since she saw him. Somehow, that gave me a glimmer of new hope.

I fell to my knees and pressed my hands together in a gesture of prayer. I forget what I said, perhaps I never knew, but words flowed from my lips in an unbroken torrent of adoration. This time, He had come. This time, He had listened to me. This time, He had answered my plea.

The crowd stood motionless, stupefied by the spectacle. Shafts of golden light fell individually upon each one of them. The walls trembled as if they too felt the warmth. Two glass chandeliers that I had not noticed before, hanging over the pews, left and right, swayed gently, catching rays of sunlight and transforming them into brightly-coloured rainbows all across the church.

Slowly, the crowd made their way back to the pews. They sat down in unison as I got to my feet. Lily returned to her chair at the long table. It was then that I saw the serpent recoiling from the cross and sliding across the floor towards me. I was not afraid, though, but regarded it as if it were a caterpillar moving between the flowers in my Garden.

That was when it happened. The change. The metamorphosis. I had seen it many times before in the Garden. The shedding of an outer skin to free another creature from within. But that was a beautiful sight. Then the creature would fly through the air with outstretched wings and come to rest on flowers which I had nurtured.

This was a very different metamorphosis. This time, the scaly outer skin fell back to free a very different kind of creature. This creature had no wings. This creature did not fly through the sky, but rested on two short, thin legs that buckled slightly under the weight of an obese body and broad, hunched shoulders, which carried a head that was large and bald. This creature belonged to a most dangerous species. This creature was a man.

He was beside me, surveying me with eyes that bulged from his twisted head.

"Handsome, aren't I?" That laugh again. "Handsome like your Adam." He paused to throw his head in the direction of the crowd as if he were looking for someone.

"What, is your husband not here to take care of you?" he sneered. "Don't tell me he abandoned you? Did you do something to upset him? Weren't you...good enough for him?"

He did not expect a response. He remembered my weaknesses too well. I despised him more than ever.

He was dressed in a long black gown that reached to the ground. In his hand, he carried a wig made of coarsely textured hair, which he placed upon his bald head.

"There! Better like that?"

He smiled at me, and I thought that I would vomit. I cast my gaze to the floor, but did not dare to close my eyes in case I missed what he did next. I would be ready for him this time.

"You!" He roared at the girl. "What's your name? Lily, isn't it?"

Lily did not reply.

"Do I make a good barrister, Lily?" He gripped the lapel of his gown close to his chest and feigned a stance of pomposity.

"Perhaps I should introduce myself," he went on, sweeping his head low in an exaggerated bow. "Madam! May I call you Lily?"

Still the girl was silent.

"Very well, then...Miss Scott. That is what they call you at the Bar, isn't it? Miss Scott, I understand that you are here to represent the Defendant. I am your opponent in this case – Counsel for the Prosecution. My name is...Mr. Sin."

Before Lily could answer him, he turned around to face me

where I now sat in my chair at the head of the table with the girl, and said:

"Forgive me, Your Honour. I forgot for a moment that I should be addressing you as the Judge in this matter. Are you ready for me to begin?"

What to do? The situation was not a new one for me – good and evil existing side by side with only me as their dividing line. I had chosen wrongly last time. Could I avoid doing so again? I thought for a moment and then said:

"If it is His will, then I am ready to hear you."

I was happy with my reply until he asked:

"His will, Your Honour? But how can you know what is His will, and what is mine?"

He had a point. How could I know? Might He not be testing me again? If only He would speak to me and tell me what to do! Why did it have to be like this, cloaked in silence?

"It is your choice, Your Honour," he continued, exploiting my hesitation. "Perhaps you would prefer to call an adjournment, return to your garden? There is plenty of time. Time is something we all have in abundance here."

"I can answer that question." It was the girl.

"There is no need for an adjournment, Mr...Sin, or may I call you Satan? That is what they call you, isn't it?"

Lily grew in confidence as she continued:

"Eve has postponed this moment for long enough. It is time for her soul to have a proper hearing. You do know what I mean by the word 'soul' don't you, Mr Sin?"

I feared for the girl's safety at that moment. She did not understand the risks she was taking in speaking to him so. I did not doubt that her wits were sharp, nor that she was more intelligent than I could ever hope to be. But what had she experienced of guile, craft, flattery, insincerity – evil? Little, I suspected. Otherwise she would not be able to sustain such optimism as I had witnessed in her. She seemed to have an innate belief that everything would turn out well in the end. And she believed what she was told; I had seen that at first hand – it had not occurred to her that I might be deceiving her when I said that room 12 was empty. She had accepted my words without hesitation, not seeking to confirm them for herself. Would that I had been more like her. Would that I had believed what He had told me, and stayed away from that deathly tree. But instead I chose to accept the words of Satan. Why? Because they were laden with compliments and sophistry and illusion.

Yes, I understand these terms now. I have not existed here for so long without learning anything from my mistakes. But what matter? It is too late for me. I seek nothing for myself anymore. And yet, if I could only protect her – Lily, then perhaps my life would not have been in vain.

He was looking at her with intent. I recognised it in his eyes, far beyond his metamorphosed state. To me, he was still a serpent, seeking out his victim, planning his attack. I even knew what he was thinking as he glared at the girl:

"Her motives are too good. I have to stop her. She is dangerous to my cause. Where shall I begin? Wherein lies her weakness? What can I exploit?"

But how could I stop him? I possessed no mastery of language to outmanoeuvre him. Without doubt, there was no chance of appealing to his better nature.

I had no time to warn her of his ways. He was about to break his silence. She had stung him by her reference to the soul and now he was ready for her. He hated that word 'soul'. It reminded him of everything he had lost. Just to know that someone was thinking it sent him into a fury of scheming to break that person down. But to chastise him with it, as the girl had done, was surely to unleash him upon a dark and sinister avenue of destruction.

"It is an interesting concept," continued Satan, "that of a soul as a Defendant. But I am afraid I do not entirely understand it. Perhaps you would be so kind as to explain it to me, Lily."

I saw the girl flinch as he pronounced her name, as if he were uttering her death sentence.

"Your ignorance surprises me, Mr Sin. Particularly as it was you who tried to capture Eve's soul from the hands of God in the first place. The battle was of your making. You recognised that He had given her freedom of will, without which her deeds would have had no capacity for moral substance. You saw, that is, that she could make choices. She was not just a physical entity made up of body parts that included a brain. She was not God's automaton. But you did not like that, did you? So you set about exploiting the freedom she had been given. You made God her judge and jury in the Garden and then you set about your prosecution of her soul. And now you find it difficult to comprehend that her soul has someone to defend it this time."

I studied him carefully all the while the girl was speaking. I noticed how he smiled at the crowd whenever she made a point which troubled him. I saw how he looked away distractedly to give the impression that he was bored and unimpressed by what she said. I watched him take out a pocket watch and place it to his ear in an attempt to break her concentration. I observed an escalating number of beads of perspiration breaking out upon his quasi-human brow the longer she went on.

When she finished speaking, he began to applaud. The girl seemed uncomfortable, perhaps a little embarrassed. He was good at creating that reaction. And it pleased him, too.

"Bravo!" He exclaimed, thinking of his next move. Then he turned to me:

"You have an excellent barrister on your side, Eve's Soul. Pity that her talents are wasted on one such as you!"

I felt tears welling up inside me as he spat out his words. He was right. The girl deserved a better cause than a soul such as mine.

Then it happened. Something strange. Something new. I heard another voice inside my head, saying:

"The girl is winning! She has got to him! He cannot vent his frustration on her, so he is searching for another outlet. That is all. Don't give up, Eve! Wait and see!"

It was Eve the Judge I was hearing. I began to understand.

34

They called it a trial. I knew what that meant. They need not have explained it to me in such detail. I used the time to observe the two of them. Wasn't that what a Judge was supposed to do?

She, so graceful, so open, so true. He, her antithesis in every way. But a Judge could not be biased, that was surely the point. Unprejudiced and objective, a true judge's role was to listen attentively to what each side had to say, and then summarize the evidence. But, there was more: a Judge, by definition, had to make a judgement. A rational, clear-headed, unequivocal, fair judgement.

Then it occurred to me: if I were to be a good judge, I would have to be like God, or as close to His likeness as it was possible for one such as me to be. Watching from my elevated position at the head of the table until the time came for me to give my judgement, to pass sentence, perhaps, on my own soul.

Was that not what He had done already, on the day he banished us, Adam and me, from Paradise? I had hoped He might not have witnessed our grave mistakes, but of course He had. He saw everything, and now I must do the same. I must be attentive to every detail, even if I did not like what I saw. Of course, it would be hard if justice obliged me to condemn my own soul. Yet how much harder it must have been for Him – to be forced to punish His own children, His Creation, those for whom He had had such high hopes and plans. Was that what He wanted of me, here, in His house, was that why He had led me here? That I might understand what it was like for Him? That I might not blame Him anymore for His harshness?

All was silent. They were ready for me. It was time for the trial to begin. Lily took her seat while Satan remained standing. I sensed an urgency in his stance, as if he had an unfinished task to complete. She seemed calm and untroubled by comparison. That was my observation. Nothing more, nothing less. It surprised me how easy I found it to put away all thoughts of hostility towards him and of tenderness towards her, especially as the contrast between them was so striking.

He began:

"Eve! First Created Woman! Mother of the Human Race!"

He pointed a finger at me as he spoke, then turned to face the crowd.

"She needs no introduction. We all know who she is. You have heard her story before."

They were studying me, all of them, searching my face for a sign of something, anything, that would make their task easier. What did they hope to find? A self-satisfied smile? A tear of remorse? Anger, bitterness, resentment? And, if I offered them nothing to seize upon, what would they read into that? That I was cold and passionless? That I was indifferent to the wrongs I had committed? That I was a lost cause?

A woman in the second row with short red hair smiled at me. I saw pity in her eyes. She wanted to believe in me. Perhaps she was thinking that she herself had made mistakes, perhaps she was congratulating herself because she had not. How long, I wondered, would it take before I let her down?

I dared not stir but sat rigid like a frightened animal before a predator hoping that immobility would render it invisible.

"Perfect, isn't she? Like a work of art."

I heard his words, but they were abstracted from me, as if they were describing someone else, someone I did not know, someone I did not wish to know. He turned to an old woman in the crowd with skin dried up with age, and continued:

"Lucky girl, don't you think? What would you give for looks like hers? See how she sits like a queen on her throne, regal, composed, unblemished by the trials of life."

I watched the woman's expression changing as he spoke to her. At first she had been curious to understand me better, mindful of the fact that at least she and I were of the same sex, and thereby capable of a mutual understanding to some degree. Although we shared the quality of being female from two opposite ends of the spectrum, it linked us nevertheless like night and day. She would listen, she would reflect, she would learn, and in her aged wisdom it would not be hard for her to make a final judgement. That was her thinking when he began to speak – I could see it in her piercing brown eyes.

But then, all changed. I became "lucky", I became "beautiful", I sat like "a queen on her throne", I was "regal", I was "composed". No longer a woman needy of her considered opinion and pragmatic assistance. I was an impostor, a violator of the bond that had served to unite us moments before. Why had she not seen it in me earlier? Had age dulled her wits as it had dimmed her eyes? I was not worthy of her wisdom. I considered myself above her in every way – how I sat erect, with chin held high, silently studying the crowd as if they were my servants. And all the while her thinking changed I remained the same.

By the time he paused for breath, she had heard enough. Her mind was made up. I had to go. She did not want to be reminded of her former opinion of me, and so she looked away – from me to him. He had won one soul, would the others follow?

"But what gives her the right to be so self-assured? What has she contributed to mankind?"

As he spoke, his gaze rested upon a young man seated at the end of the pew beside the door. His hair was dark and long to his shoulders, and his skin was pale and unblemished with just a suggestion of manhood in the shadow on his chin. When he realised that Satan was looking at him, he turned from him to face the floor. He was nervous, afraid. He had heard of us both and he did not want to risk losing his innocence to him the way I had. He would block out his words and pay no attention to me. That way he would be safe and his soul untouched.

Too late. He had heard him before he could prevent it: I was self-assured. I had contributed nothing to mankind. The words made him shift edgily in his seat. He crossed his arms tightly over his chest. He longed to be more confident, self-assured. It had probably been his greatest wish on Earth. But it had been beyond his reach. Instead, he had satisfied himself with being young and naïve but good at heart. He strove for what was best. He always wanted to do the right thing. Yet, what had he contributed to mankind? He was asking himself the question as he raised his eyes in my direction for the first time. I had seen that same thought often in my Abel's eyes – I could not be mistaken. They had both been taken too young. Why, God?

Did they not deserve the opportunity to fulfil themselves, achieve their aims, prove to the world, and more importantly, to themselves, that they were valuable human beings?

The young man saw these thoughts in me, for they were his too. Satan had not won this soul.

"Every one of you has suffered in your life. Am I right?"

His eyes passed hungrily from row to row.

"You did not deserve to suffer."

He lowered his voice until it was the whisper of a confidante.

"You are all good people. You would not be here if it were otherwise. None of you chose to suffer pain. Your lives should have been filled with happiness and joy, as Eve's was. She had everything – a loving husband, a beautiful environment in which to live a trouble-free life. She was not burdened by the problems of your lives: illness, debts, hard labour…death. None of those were meant to be. She brought them about. She caused them by her selfish desire to better herself."

His voice grew loud and climactic. It sent a shiver down my spine.

"She was not content to be God's Chosen One, Mother of Mankind. That was not good enough for her. She wanted to be God. She thought she deserved Godly knowledge. She believed herself to be greater than the angels who protected her. She thought she had a right to know. Never mind that God had told her that such knowledge was forbidden to her. What did it matter what He said? He was only the fool who had created her in the first place. SHE would decide what she wanted to do. And no-one would stop her, not even Him!"

The church was hot with the vehemence of his words. They hung over the crowd like an electric thunderstorm. No-one dared to stir, not even Lily. She sat transfixed as if the magnitude of her undertaking would overpower her. But I was the Judge, not Lily. Yet, what to do? Call a halt to the proceedings? Give my judgement now? Spare us all the torment of his venom? It was my decision alone.

"Enough!" I cried, "We have heard enough! Please stop now!"

It was all I could think to say. I had no plan. There was no motive behind my words.

"Do you mean to say that the Judge is ready to give her verdict?"

I should have guessed that this would be his response and prepared for it. But I was not quick enough for him. In any case, wasn't I ready? I made to give him my answer when suddenly another voice was speaking. It came from behind me. I could not see him, but his identity was unmistakable. It was Michael.

"This is a Court of Justice, Mr. Sin," he said quietly. "Where would be the justice in a verdict given before the Defence had had an opportunity to respond?"

I could see him now. He was beside me. I wished he would sweep me up as he had once done and fly away with me, far, far from here. Not this time, Eve, I said to myself. Michael smiled down at me as if he read my thought, and then he spoke again, to Lily this time.

"We are ready for you, Lily."

217

35

She looked young and vulnerable as she got to her feet, the girl. Was she up to the task they had set her? I doubted it at that moment. What chance would she have against a powerful force of destruction such as he?

She pushed her hair behind her ears and began:

"I am representing Eve's soul here today because I chose to do so. It was not pre-determined that I should be here. I was offered a choice and I exercised the freedom of will which God gave me – gave every one of us – and I decided that this was something I wanted to do."

She paused and I feared that her concentration may have been broken, but then she went on:

"Why did I want to represent her? That is a difficult question to answer."

She glanced over at me as if to remind herself of the reason.

"I am a barrister. I have been trained to think as a barrister. I enjoy a challenge and I have been taught that every one of us is entitled to a fair hearing. I am a mouthpiece for those who are unable to speak persuasively, articulately for themselves. In other words, Eve needed me and I rose to the intellectual challenge. Not a very noble reason, is it?"

She paused for a moment to appeal to the crowd. She had their attention, every one of them.

"Where is the moral virtue in a motive like that? A game of chess, a battle of wits, an egotistical desire to outwit the opponent, regardless of the strength of your case?"

So it was as I had feared. The girl had used me. I was a player on her stage as I had been a puppet on His. That was all I had ever been. Why hope for more? It was what I deserved.

"And then I met her. I was intrigued. I wanted to learn as much as I could about the woman who was to be my most famous client. No doubt you understand how I felt. I have seen it in every one of you – the desire to know more, the curiosity in one such as she, the need to identify in order to understand, the fear that you would make the wrong decision."

So she had seen it in them, too.

"But I had an advantage over you all. I was able to talk to Eve. I was given the opportunity to get to know her. It was not difficult. For she was more like me than I had expected her to be. She will be surprised to hear me say that, for she thinks we are worlds apart."

Lily looked towards me again and smiled.

"She the unintelligent, unsophisticated child of nature, I the educated, worldly barrister, a product of the twenty-first century. Quick-witted, articulate, knowledgeable, hot-tempered, expressive."

It was as if she had looked into my head and read my innermost thoughts. And I had not even noticed!

"And yet, I knew her so very well. She was curious. She was interested in everything around her. She wanted to know more, to extend the boundaries of her understanding. And how she has suffered for the gift of an enquiring mind!"

She stopped to collect her thoughts. She was uncertain how much to tell without breaking an unspoken confidence.

"You have heard eloquently from my learned friend of the sins she committed. To put it bluntly, Eve ate from the tree of the knowledge of good and evil, a tree which God had forbidden to her. Why was it forbidden, perhaps you will ask. And thereby you will be guilty of the very same crime for which Eve has punished herself for an eternity. She committed the sin of asking "Why?"

Ah, but she went further than asking, she chose to act in order to find out, some of you will be saying. Is that a crime? Is it truly less of a sin to think of an action than to carry it out? Is not the sin in the thinking of it? If indeed it is a sin in the first place. Perhaps the Prosecution is better placed to answer questions on that subject, for it was Mr. Sin who chose to tempt Eve in the Garden of Eden. He was subtle, he used argument, persuasive argument, like a true barrister, to convince the trusting, naïve Eve that she would not be committing a wrong if she ate the fruit. After all, God had determined to give his children Adam and Eve freewill in order that their actions might possess true moral value rather than being actions which had no more worth than those of an automaton. It was His decision that they should exercise their capacity for choice. Of course, He hoped that they would make the right choices, the good, morally valuable choices that He so loves. Yet He did not explain to them what was right and what was wrong. He expected them to obey His word without them understanding what the consequences of their actions would be."

Lily paused for breath. She feared she was talking for too long. Was she losing their attention? Should she wind up her submissions and hope for the best? The faces of the crowd told her that she had time left, and so she went on:

"Perhaps He underestimated the first woman He had created? Perhaps her curiosity exceeded even His expectations? We are told that He punished them, Adam and Eve. They were expelled from their Paradise and the rest of us have been searching for it ever since. But it's hard to find, isn't it? You have all looked for it in your time, but how many of you have found it for longer than a fleeting moment?"

It was not a rhetorical question, she asked it of each member of the congregation in turn with her eyes. Not one of them put up a hand.

"Elusive, Paradise, isn't it? She lost it for us all. That is what Mr. Sin would have us believe. In its place, we are given toil, burden, pain and last of all, death, the greatest curse of all. God's punishment for Eve's wrongs. Satan had proved that every one of us is corruptible. He had won."

I was confused. Had Lily forgotten whose side she was on? Had Satan somehow got to her too?

"But what if God's punishment was not a punishment at all? What if He anticipated Eve's actions? Anticipation would not make her actions determined; it would only mean that He was omniscient. The choice would still have been hers. Just as it was mine to be here today, and yours too, all of you here for whatever reason you are locked in Purgatory."

"Objection!"

Satan's voice thundered through the church like an avalanche, shaking the pews and the concentration of the people.

221

"Your Honour, this is pure speculation! My submissions were based entirely upon the facts as we know them. My learned friend is merely speculating on what might or might not have been in God's head."

He addressed himself entirely to me. I confess I was divided at that moment. I, Eve the Defendant, wanted to shout out, "So you are afraid, Mr. Sin. You see what it is like to be losing control! Where will your failure take you next?" On the other hand, Eve the Judge was thinking, "You are right, Mr. Sin. Lily is speculating on something she cannot prove."

"Miss Scott," I tried to sound as authoritative as I could. "I have to ask you to be more..." I could not think of the right word to use.

"Specific?" asked Lily.

"Yes, specific," I replied.

"I apologise, Your Honour. The point I wanted to make was this: Eve was given freewill, Eve exercised her freewill in the making of a choice, Eve chose to eat from a tree from which God had forbidden her to eat, God did not explain to her why it was forbidden, Eve was tempted by Satan who implemented sophisticated argument to persuade her that she was not doing wrong, Eve is the possessor of an enquiring mind, Eve's motives were not evil, we are told that God punished mankind for Eve's wrongdoing, God is a fair and just God, God would not punish anyone unfairly. The question then remains, did God punish Eve fairly, or did He not punish her at all? I have sought to argue that the sort of punishment which we are led to believe that God imposed upon Eve and all mankind would be too harsh a punishment given the background of the crime. I argue, therefore that God did not punish us at all. Eve

222

was not punished. Adam was not punished. None of us were punished."

I could not prevent myself from interposing. The argument was too important for me to avoid. I spoke identically as Eve the Defendant and Eve the Judge when I asked:

"Then why were we banished from Paradise?"

"You can answer that question for yourself, Eve."

"I? How?"

"You can tell us what happened when you left your Garden of Eden."

Where should I start? I did not like to hear my own voice for too long. I preferred to hear the girl explain me to the crowd in her own words. But she had asked, and I owed her this much. So I spoke:

"We clung to each other like the branches of an olive tree, my husband and I. We were novices, children in a universe we did not comprehend. Adam knew more than I and so I followed his command, especially as I had so recently failed in that respect. He told me that we were to leave behind everything we had held dear up to then and start again in another land. We were led away by angels whom God had sent to watch over us."

I glanced over my shoulder in the direction I knew that I would find Michael listening carefully to every word I uttered.

"It was a difficult time. The land was hard, arid, not beautiful like Eden. We worked most hours God gave us with little reward. And we argued. How we argued in those early days. Like wild animals. Adam no longer trusted me the way he once had. I could see in his eyes that he blamed me for our new situation. My only consolation lay in our dear son Abel. I suffered so much pain in order to give him life. Childbirth was a

223

bitter-sweet experience, but it was worthwhile to see my Abel's loving face look up at me."

I smiled to myself and was silent for a moment before I went on:

"You cannot imagine how much we suffered when he was taken from us. That he died at the hand of his own brother, born of the same blood as he, and loved in the same way, was almost too much for a mother to bear. Almost, because I somehow survived his death. Had I caused his sin too? Did it grow from the seed of my wrongdoing? I have often asked myself that question. But I have no answer. I am not a scholar. There is little I understand. I wish it would be otherwise. There is much I would like to understand.

Strangely, suffering brought us closer together, Adam and me. We learnt what was important in a way which we had never experienced in Paradise. We told each other what mattered, we gave each other comfort, we learnt from our mistakes. Gradually Adam trusted me again. How happy that made me to earn his trust rather than to take it for granted as I had done in Eden!

When he died, I told myself that God had kept His greatest punishment until last. I could have borne any other with Adam by my side, but without him, I was empty inside. I was spent. Death was the hardest lesson of all. It was the one thing I could never forgive myself for, however much I replayed the past. I could not look at it any other way than something which I could have avoided for my family and myself. By the time my Adam had gone, death had lost its sting. There was nothing left to harm me but existence itself.

Suddenly, I longed for death, for a state of nothingness in

which I could be free finally to forget. But it was not to be. God's lessons were not complete. He brought me here, and still I could not forget.

Then the girl came. Lily. I was told she was coming, but it did not matter to me. Why should it? The only people I wanted to see had not been here to greet me. No doubt they had gone on to a better life which they deserved.

She made me curious. I remembered the part of me that longed to understand. Suddenly I wondered whether I might be capable of knowing more. Not just about where I was and why I was here, but who I was and what mattered to me still. Before she came, I would not allow myself to express my emotions. Anger was something I kept locked away inside me. She showed me how to let it out. And when I saw her lying so still and pale in that bed, I wanted to cry for her and protect her as if she were my child."

"What bed?" Lily's voice was almost a whisper but it brought me back to the present. Oh God, why did You have to make me so clumsy with words?

"Lying in what bed?"

I knew she would not let go of the question now it had been asked. No matter that we were in the middle of a trial in which I was supposed to be the Judge. And Satan would not intervene, of that I could be certain.

"I saw you lying in a bed in the room at the top of the stairs."

"You mean the room which you stopped me from entering?"

I reddened. The trial no longer mattered to me. Would she understand that?

"Yes, that room. I wanted to save you from anxiety. I was afraid for you, Lily."

225

"But how could I have been in that room when I was speaking to you outside it? I never went in. It could not have been me. Say it wasn't me!"

What to do? I could not lie to the girl. Yet, I did not entirely understand it myself. I could only guess. As could Lily. I saw the thought come over her face. I could not protect her from it. What would she do now? Cry? Shout? Run from the church back to the room?

I could never predict what the girl would do.

"We have a trial to finish," she said quietly, as if it were Michael speaking. "Shall we continue?"

"I have no more to add. You asked me to describe what happened when we left the Garden of Eden and I have told you in the only way I know. But nothing I have said answers the question I asked of you, why were we banished from Paradise if not in order to punish us?"

At first I thought that Lily was not going to speak, she remained silent for so long. Finally she raised her head, looked hard into my eyes and said, as if I were the only other person in the church:

"Eve! Don't you see? You have answered your own question. Think on it, Eve! God sent you away from Paradise in order that you might learn, that we might all learn. You and Adam were like children, as you said, before then. After that, you grew together through your suffering, you learnt to have a deeper understanding of one another, you loved each other in the midst of your difficulties. How much more satisfying than a love that survives in the midst of easy times. It is not hard for a love to exist in Paradise. But through trials and tragedies and degradation, that is another matter."

226

"Then why did He take my Abel and Adam away from me? Surely you will not argue that that was not punishment?"

I was crying like a baby as I spoke through my sobs, but I did not care. Let them all think what they would of me, it did not concern me. What mattered were my questions and Lily's answers. Nothing else.

"I can only give you my opinion, Eve. I may be wrong. But what I believe is this: you had learnt what lessons He had chosen that you might learn if you chose to do so also. And it was time for you to move on in another direction. You had something else to learn which perhaps Adam had already learnt. You needed to have a fuller understanding of yourself. Not as part of a couple – the couple – Adam and Eve, but as Eve, the woman. And there was a great deal to learn, Eve. Do not underestimate yourself any longer."

"Congratulations, Miss Scott! An excellent performance if I may say so. Especially from one who is supposed to be lying dead in a bed!"

His applause grated on us as much as his words. When would he go away? Would he always be here to torment us? I needed to speak. It was my duty as the Judge, after all.

"Have you anything to add in closing before I give my judgement, Mr. Sin?"

My voice was stronger than I had heard it for a long, long time. Lily noticed it too. I could tell by the way she turned and looked at me. And so did he.

"Just this: we have heard my learned friend's somewhat emotive submissions and her conclusion appears to be that Eve's punishment is not evidence of any wrongdoing having been committed by her client. Indeed, she goes so far as to say

227

that a fair and just God would not seek to punish someone who has chosen to ignore His commands. My response to this curious line of argument is that Eve was indeed punished, as she herself seems to admit when not coaxed otherwise by her counsel. Furthermore, I submit that she was correctly punished for a sin so great that all mankind has suffered as a result. For that sin the Defendant should be retained in Purgatory for all eternity, or alternatively she should be driven to the gates of Hell where she will finally be able to rid herself of her memories once and for all. I undertake to see to that personally."

It was the young man I had seen before who was the first to rise to his feet.

"I say her soul should be freed. Eve has suffered enough!"

"She has committed no more wrong than any one of us. And less than many!" The woman with short red hair called out.

Before long, all of them were standing, crying out on my behalf. I had never experienced anything like it before. My only fear was that it was Lily who they were really cheering for, not me. I looked around me, uncertain what would happen next. There was Lily standing before them, silent and composed. Behind me stood Michael, arms held out in a gesture of mighty victory. But where was Mr. Sin? I searched the church for a sign of him, but he was nowhere to be seen. It was as if he had never existed. But how could he disappear before he had heard my judgement? The trial was not yet over.

"It is over for him," said Michael.

36

They were waiting for me to speak, all of them, quietly urging me on. I was terrified in case I let them down. I remembered how it felt to disappoint those who had placed their faith in me. I did not want to see that same look in their eyes as I had witnessed in Adam's. I must be careful, I told myself. I must think before I utter a word. Satan may have made himself invisible somehow, but I had no doubt that he was still there, listening and waiting for another opportunity.

I stood up. The floor seemed to sway beneath my feet. I clasped hold of the arm of the chair in an attempt to steady myself. No-one must see my uncertainty. I must be strong like the girl. See how she stood! So must I stand also. I let go of the chair and held my hands together before me. The posture made me feel more dignified, composed. I took a step forward towards the crowd and began to speak:

"I must address you all now. That is my duty as Judge. Forgive me if I am not clear sometimes. I am unused to speaking in this way."

My voice was faltering – had they noticed? I cleared my throat and went on, louder than before:

"I have heard the opinions of some of you. I have seen the response of you all. It touched my soul when I believed that my soul was beyond salvation. But I must not forget – and neither must you – that it is my soul that is on trial in this case, and that in giving my judgement, I must abstract myself from that soul and respond rationally and objectively to what I have heard from Counsel for both sides."

But could I? I looked towards Lily for confirmation. She nodded back at me compassionately. Poor girl! I think she hoped for more from me than I was capable of achieving. If I were to give my judgement at all, it would be simple and to the point. Not the kind of judgement that she was accustomed to hearing.

Judgement. How weighted a word! To play God and judge the actions of another was harsh enough, but to have to judge one's own soul, surely that was asking for too much?

I knew I had sinned. I had never tried to hide that. On the contrary, the fact had preyed upon my mind to the exclusion of all else. Every word that Satan had uttered against me could have been my own. Even before I came here, to this emptiness called Purgatory, I had already passed judgement upon myself for the wrongs I had done, both to my soul and to mankind.

It surprised me at first that I remained here. Why did He not see fit to throw me out? Satan had already taken me for his own. It never occurred to me that I might still have a purpose to fulfil. His purpose. The girl planted that idea in my mind. Not deliberately. Not even consciously. But gradually. She showed me an alternative way of existing, stronger than my own, truer to oneself. Wilful, brave, compassionate, thoughtful. For the very first time since I left Eden, I wondered whether there might be more for me to achieve.

Perhaps I was mistaken. Perhaps I was done. Perhaps I read more into Lily's presence here than I should.

"The choice is yours, Eve!"

It was Lily's voice I heard. Had she read my thoughts, or was she encouraging me to go on with my judgement? Either way, she was right. The choice was mine.

"I have listened carefully to what both sides have said. It was not an easy task, particularly as the decision that I now make will have an impact on the rest of my existence."

Why had He given me this to do? What was He hoping for? He knew what choice I had made long ago. He and His messengers had seen for themselves how I chose to exist, hidden away in my small garden with no one to disturb me and only my books and my thoughts for company. If death as a finality were to be denied me, I swore that I would create it myself; He was too generous in offering me an opportunity to rectify the wrongs I had committed – I did not deserve another chance.

At least, I convinced myself that that was my motive for remaining here in Purgatory. But was it my true motive? I had to think clearly and truthfully now, like the girl. This was likely to be my last chance.

I closed my eyes to shut them all out, even Lily. I must not be influenced by any of them now. It was dark again. There was no sound. I likened my state to a birth: I was fighting for survival from within a place I could not understand; my instincts were forcing me on; soon, if all went well, I would be breathing for myself for the very first time.

Why had I chosen to stay here, living a death for every moment that I existed? The question went round and round in my head like a bird trapped in a chimney. Was it for His sake, or for my own?

Slowly my answer came to me: it had suited me to believe that I was finally acting for unselfish reasons. So ignorant had I been that I had not realised that I was deluding myself. It was not His will that I was choosing to protect; it was my own. I was afraid that I would be let down again, raised to great heights only to be dropped. Just as I had been when I was banished from Paradise, just as I had been when Abel had been taken from me, then my Adam. Just as I had been when death had carried me on Michael's wings to a new earthless existence, which I had believed would contain those I had lost.

I would protect myself from hurt, I had determined. And until the girl arrived – Lily – I had believed that I had succeeded and that there was no other way for me to exist.

And now? What did I truly believe now? They were waiting for me: the crowd, Lily, Michael, Satan and God, each of them hoping that my way would be theirs. But what was my way, Eve's way?

I opened my eyes, ready at last to address them all:

"Satan was right. I sinned. To be accurate, my soul sinned, the Defendant. And it was no ordinary sin. My sin was so great that the whole world suffered as a result, and no doubt will continue to suffer for eternity. I changed a course of events. I showed that His will does not dictate our actions. I showed that we all have a choice.

I do not mean to sound proud of that fact. I do not say it to favour the Defendant. On the contrary, I say it because I recognise that I made the wrong choice. He was not responsible for my actions, I was. And it is only fair that I should suffer as a result."

I returned to my chair and sat down again in order to give myself time to think what to say next. Michael was standing where he had been before. He seemed anxious, perhaps even a little afraid. I did not want to disappoint him, he had fought so hard for my soul. But the decision was mine, I had to do what I thought right.

"But that was not the end. It could have been the end for me. But He chose otherwise. Why did He not cast me down there and then? I have asked myself that question and I have no answer. Lily's answer would be this: 'A quest for knowledge is not a wrong in itself. God must have recognised that. Perhaps He underestimated the curiosity of His first created woman. Perhaps He anticipated Eve's actions. Perhaps He did not punish Eve at all. Perhaps He had more for Eve to learn if she so chose. Perhaps she had not yet fulfilled her purpose.'

Is she right, the girl? Is there still a purpose for me to fulfil? If there is, then would it not be wrong for me, the Judge, to condemn my soul and remove that possibility?

But, if she is wrong, and Satan is right, then why should I grant my soul the opportunity of another chance? Might that not cause more harm to mankind?"

I did not ask my questions in order that someone would answer them for me. I never expected a response. I only asked them of myself, that in so doing I might be able to formulate my own conclusion.

Therefore, when a voice in the crowd echoed through the church towards me I was stunned into a sudden silence as I searched the many faces for its creator. I did not have to look far. It was an old man in the front row, whom I had noticed before. I had not heard him speak until now, but he had nodded encouragingly towards me throughout the trial.

"Let it be, Eve!" he said quietly, as if his words were meant only for me. "Let it be!"

It was as if a thousand heavy chains had dropped from my heart, melted away by a million years of sunshine all at once. I fixed my gaze on the old man as if I feared that if I did not do so he might disappear. Was I so blind that I had not seen what existed before my very eyes? Could it be that my ears had transported me where my sight had failed?

There was only one word I was capable of uttering:

"Adam!"

Part Four

ABEL

37

I dreamt I saw my mother in a land I did not know. It was a beautiful place, filled with flowers of every colour of the rainbow. My mother was walking between them, careful not to disturb a single one. She stopped occasionally and stooped to pull out the weeds that were growing around them.

The day was gold with sunshine, warm, nurturing sunshine. My mother was alone. She was smiling. She was happy.

Next, I was walking towards her along a path that wound between trees stooping with their heavy load of fruit. She seemed glad to see me and smiled and waved at me as if she had not seen me for a long time. I was happy to see her too, and ran the short distance between us until my mother was able to lift me up in her strong arms and swing me around and around and around.

"My son," she laughed, "your father and I were looking for you. Where have you been?"

"I was by the lake," I replied, "with my friend."

"Ah, your secret friend!" she sighed. "Will I never get to meet him?"

"He says he knows you already," I answered sternly, as if she should have known.

We carried on walking along the path together, and presently we were joined by my father.

"Abel!" He said, looking from my mother to me. "Where have you been?"

"He was by the lake with his secret friend," my mother replied.

"When do I get to meet your friend?" My father enquired with a smile.

"He says he knows you already," I snapped at him, angered that I should be asked the same question again.

Then they exchanged a glance, an adult glance, that I did not understand, and my mother asked:

"What else does your friend tell you?"

"He said that you were fulfilling your purpose."

That surprised her, and my father. They had not expected such a grown-up response. Suddenly they wanted to know more.

"My purpose?" My mother repeated the words as if she had not properly heard them.

"Yes. Your purpose."

"What purpose is that?"

It was clear that she wanted a precise answer. I thought for a moment, anxious to recollect my friend's exact words, then I said:

"To advocate for the souls of those who need your help."

They were truly astonished now, but they did not seem cross, so I went on:

"He said that he had guided you towards that purpose, but that you had not always realised it."

That made my mother look sad, and I wondered whether I had said too much. So I stopped speaking. But my father encouraged me to go on. He took my hand in his and squeezed it tightly:

"Abel," he said, "there is much that you do not yet understand."

"He said the same of you!" I replied, "Although you have already learnt a great deal. How was it that he described you? Wiser than before. You know how to be patient. You have remembered how to listen."

My father seemed happy with the description and he laughed. But strangely, there were tears in his eyes at the same time. I had never seen my father cry.

Then my mother handed him a beautiful silk handkerchief. The colour was a vivid part of the dream. It was lilac.

"Use this," she said to him tenderly, and he wiped away his tears.

It was then that I remembered. I was angry with myself for not having remembered sooner.

"He told me to tell you something," I said to my mother. I could see from her face that she was eager to know what it was that my friend had said.

"He said to tell you that you had made the right choice."

She was happy with that, so I continued:

"And so did she."

"She?"

"Your friend."

"My friend?"

"Yes. She had not understood her purpose either, until you helped her. She thought she was somewhere where she was not. You showed her that she was wherever she chose to be. And the place where she wanted to be – she was there all the time!"

The dream grew hazy after that, as if a cloudy white vapour

was gathering me up. But there was something else I had to tell my mother before I woke up. I forced the dream to remain long enough to turn to her and say it:

"He wants you to know that he thinks your name suits you – Lily, beautiful, like the flower."